LOVE, HEARTBREAK, AND A ST

T0267582

Such a Winter's Day

SUSAN WHITE

30 YEARS

ACORNPRESS

*Celebrating thirty years of
Island stories and voices.*

Praise for Susan White

Praise for *Skyward*

Set in an entirely believable near future, the story of Emery, Daisy and the other Lesser Thans is as unsettling as it is uplifting, as sweet as it is gritty.

—Carla Gunn, *Author of Amphibian*

Praise for *Waiting for Stillwater*

While there appears to be plenty of emotional storylines occurring (and I haven't touched on them all), the narrative is never convoluted nor challenging to follow. Ms. White deliberately lets the story unfurl, and the backstories of each character are revealed in due time. Rachel appears to have returned at the right moment for her own peace of mind and she also acts as the catalyst for the story, uniting everyone and in the process, assists them to cope as well finding what she came back to Amelia's for. Indeed, Waiting for Still Water comes full circle and as such is a satisfying and captivating read for any age, much like her 2015 book The Memory Chair was.

— James Fisher, Miramichi Reader

Praise for *The Year Mrs. Montague Cried*

The novel takes readers through a painful process of grief, acceptance, and then finally courage when faced with death. Taylor's journal is a moving account of her difficult year in which she learns to accept her brother's illness and to deal with the tension and strain in her relationships with her parents, her brother, and her relatives. Highly Recommended.

—Alicia Cheng, Vancouver Public Library, Vancouver BC

Praise for *Fear of Drowning*

I have previously reviewed two of Ms. White's books, *The Memory Chair* (2015) and *Waiting for Still Water* (2016), both of which I enjoyed very much. While some of her titles may be considered "Young Adult" she recently informed me that: "in my mind, the YA/adult distinction is more about marketing than readership." That may be true, for Ms. White's stories (at least the ones I have read) have an ageless readability about them. They neither "dumb down" nor unnecessarily sophisticate the written word, making the reader feel ignorant or unschooled. What she does best is write a good story, with characters that are crisply defined. *Fear of Drowning* is no different.

—James Fisher, Mirimachi Reader

Praise for *The Wright Retreat*

If you've ever been on a writing retreat, *The Wright Retreat* will ring true. There are the people who just can't get started, the ones who have spent their lives thinking they should write their story and are finally getting around to it, and the ones who already have published but are in a rut.

More importantly, they are all in some way damaged by their past—abusive partners, mistreatment at residential school and at the hands of nuns running a home for pregnant teens, debilitating anxiety, and relationships that have changed or ended. And as the characters come to grips with their traumas, the awful history of the retreat location itself is revealed.

"Life comes with layers and layers of pain. And healing is hard work," says one of the characters in *The Wright Retreat*. "You have to wait, be patient, and be willing to let the deep wound heal right to the core. Some folks aren't able to do the work."

—Philip Moscovitch, Atlantic Books Today

While this is a work of fiction, the content in this book includes intense discussion on homophobia, sexual assault, violence and substance abuse.

Printed in Canada

Cover: Tracy Belsher
Design: Rudi Tusek
Editor: Penelope Jackson

Library and Archives Canada Cataloguing in Publication

Title: Such a winters' day : love, heartbreak, and a story of acceptance / Susan White.
Names: White, Susan, 1956- author
Identifiers: Canadiana (print) 20240459431 | Canadiana (ebook) 20240459458 | ISBN 9781773661766
  (softcover) | ISBN 9781773661773 (EPUB)
Subjects: LCGFT: Novels.
Classification: LCC PS8645.H5467 S83 2024 | DDC C813/.6—dc23

The publisher acknowledges the support of the Government of Canada, the Canada Council for the Arts and the Province of Prince Edward Island for our publishing program.

ACORNPRESS

P.O. Box 22024
Charlottetown, Prince Edward Island
C1A 9J2
acornpresscanada.com

To Peter "Evan" McArthur
Feb 25, 1979—Jan 7, 2024

November 2, 2021

H ank walked slowly through King's Square. The midmorning sun was bright but the wind biting. The trees surrounding the bandstand were bare, the ground carpeted with the colourful foliage that had graced the square into late October. City workers had turned off the fountain, cleaned up the gardens, and removed the hanging baskets in preparation for winter. Fewer people were milling about, but the clusters of pigeons remained. A few were pecking wildly at a Tim Horton's paper bag. Hank felt for the gift card in the pocket of his parka. Someone had handed it to him several days ago as he stood on the corner in front of the CIBC bank, but he hadn't tried to use it yet. He hated the way heads turned toward him when he walked in the door.

Even when he hadn't been technically homeless, it was as if he wore a sign announcing his worthlessness when he entered Tim's. He'd always had enough change to pay for whatever he ordered, but the doubt and distrust were written on the servers' faces. Sometimes, the person behind the counter looked too young to be employed, and sometimes, too old to still be working at a job barely paying minimum wage. Hank tried not to judge either way. But Hank felt judged by everyone around him. Strangely, this came from a feeling of not being seen by those who passed him, while at the same time feeling each stare or passing glance as a condemnation.

The woman he'd helped up off the sidewalk a few minutes ago used the word *invisible*. Others walked by, giving the collapsed woman a wide berth, chalking up her stumble off the curb and her bleeding face to a drunken state, and not one they wished to engage with.

"Apparently, I'm invisible," the woman muttered as Hank helped her to her feet. "I'm Pearl."

Hank reached into his pocket for an unused, folded napkin and handed it to Pearl. "I'm Hank. Your face is bleeding. Are you okay?"

"They think I'm drunk. I'm not drunk," Pearl said, dabbing at her forehead. "These people walk by me every day, but they don't even see me. Not a nod or, God forbid, a kind word. I watch them scurry along, living their busy, important lives. Not one would have a clue where I live or anything about me. I'm just some scary old lady to them. That's if they even notice me. And I guess falling on these uneven, poorly maintained sidewalks makes ignoring me even easier. We're all drunks or drug addicts as far as they're concerned."

Hank sensed the anger in Pearl's words and recognized the underlying hurt. A few days ago, he'd stood on the sidewalk watching workers haul out all the furniture, fixtures, appliances, and discarded possessions from the rooming house on Duke Street. Everything was thrown in the dumpster as the pompous real estate agent stood smiling for the camera while handing the keys to the new owner.

1958

Hank hurried across King's Square. The building looked pretty much as he remembered it from when, as a boy, he'd come to Saturday matinees with George. It cost a nickel to get in, and just a dime would get you a bag of popcorn and a fountain drink. It never mattered what was playing; the fun was getting on the bus with George at the corner of Main and Douglas and getting off at the bottom of King Street, running up the hill, crossing Charlotte Street and seeing the marquee of the Capitol Theatre.

A box-shaped structure was above the doors instead of the moon-shaped Capitol Theatre sign Hank remembered, and large letters declared the building to now be the Full Gospel Assembly. An open Bible flanked by large crosses topped the gaudy sign. Hank pulled open the door and entered, envisioning the lobby as it had been when he and George rushed in to buy their tickets.

As he opened the inner doors, the loud chords of the pipe organ music and the congregation rising to their feet jolted Hank back to the present. He was late for the eleven o'clock service, but if he could find Tanya's family and slide into the row beside them during the singing, it might not be as obvious. People were waving outstretched arms and swaying their bodies. George had warned him this would be unlike any Anglican service he'd been to before.

"Those Pentecostals are nuts. They wail and whoop and holler. *Talking in tongues*, they call it, whatever that is, but it's no stuffy Church of England service, I can tell you that. How did you get messed up with that crowd?"

Hank didn't see George very often these days. George's grandmother still lived in the house next door, but George was working on a fishing boat with his uncle in Grand Manan. When he'd been home last weekend, though, it felt like old times when they hung out. Hank had almost told

George about Tanya but hadn't wanted to ruin the night. It had taken him months to even tell George he was dating anyone.

Hank had barely noticed Tanya Bennett in the first two years of high school other than the fact that she wore her long hair swooped up in a big bun and her dresses were almost to her ankles, causing her to stand out from the other girls with their Twiggy cuts and miniskirts. Hank sported the typical blue jeans rolled up at the cuffs and the tight white T-shirt. He slicked his hair back every morning with a liberal glob of Brylcreem and attempted to look like all the other guys.

And this year, even though Hank's seat in Biology was right behind Tanya Bennett's, they hadn't spoken a word to one another until the day in early December when Tanya walked right up to Hank's locker and asked him to the Sadie Hawkins dance. By Christmas, Tanya and Hank were going steady. After that everything changed, the most noticeable being Tanya's hairstyle, fashion choices, and ear piercings. But those changes were nothing compared to the big, life-altering change Tanya planned on telling her parents about at Sunday dinner today. She'd assured Hank that his coming to church would make that easier.

Hank squeezed in beside Tanya just as the congregation took their seats again. He looked toward the front, wishing to see Roy Rogers come on the large screen that once was there. And more than that he wished it was George he was sitting down beside.

November 2, 2021

Pearl Jennings limped up the stairs of her building. Walking into the vestibule, she saw her landlord on a stepladder, replacing the ceiling lightbulb.

"Good morning, Tim," Pearl called out as she pulled flyers from her mail slot.

"What happened to your face, Pearl?"

"Oh, I took a little tumble on the sidewalk. I'm fine."

"Sorry, this light's been out for a while, and I haven't forgotten about your bathroom floor. It's on the list."

"No problem. I know you've got lots on your plate."

Tim stepped down, folded up the ladder, and leaned it against the wall. He zipped up his jacket before picking up his tool pouch. "Everyone thinks we're the bad guys. They call rent increases "highway robbery," even though the cost of everything has gone through the roof. Property taxes have doubled and don't even get me started about the cost of heating fuel. There's no money in this racket, but what choice do I have? I'm not turning folks like you out on the street. And don't worry, I'm not raising your rent. I'm not the bastard everyone thinks I am."

"Now, who thinks you're a bastard?"

"Well, I'm sure those poor buggers we evicted from the place I just bought on Duke Street don't think too highly of me. That old building is a gem with great potential. And if I can turn it into four, high-end condos, I can afford to keep the other buildings I have that give tenants like you a decent place to live."

Pearl touched her throbbing cheek and realized it was still bleeding. "Take care," she called as she quickly made her way up the stairs.

"Yeah, you too, Pearl. No more falls, eh?"

Pearl walked to her door and turned the key in the lock. *Home sweet home,* she thought as she entered her small apartment. Kicking off her boots she quickly made her way into the bathroom, careful to step over the curled-up section of vinyl flooring. She grabbed a facecloth and began wiping the blood off her face.

A decent place to live, thought Pearl as she came out into her tiny kitchen and set the kettle on the stove. She'd get a roll of duct tape on her next trip to Giant Tiger and fix the bathroom floor herself. All she needed was to fall in her own bathroom, hit her head on the tub, and die. God knows how long she'd lie there before her stinking corpse would get anyone's attention.

1958

"Stop your crying, Pearl Girl. Don't know why you have to cut up such a fuss. If you would just do what you're told. Not that I ever did what my old man told me to do. And believe me, kid, my old man's belt hurt a lot worse than the palm of my hand ever will. How about we go to the Riv and get you a treat?"

Pearl wiped her tears and grabbed her red coat from the hall tree, trying to drown out her mother's angry voice.

"She thinks she's a little princess in her ugly red coat, and for some reason she thinks you're a king. A king, all right, a king of this rat-infested castle with your gold coins spent on liquor and whores, but enough pennies left to take that little bitch out for french fries. What about the rest of us?"

Pearl felt the roughness of her father's hand as he clasped hers tighter before crossing Charlotte Street. The massive, rough, hardworking hands that had beat her bare bum just minutes before. And now he was taking her to the Riviera for fries and gravy.

Pearl stepped back while Daddy opened the big door. He bowed and swooped his hand as if he were a footman welcoming royalty to a fancy dining hall.

"Enter, your Highness."

Pearl laughed and stepped inside, walking to the red leather stools at the end of the counter. "Our stools," her father always said, acting as if Walter Jennings and his daughter Pearl were the only people to ever sit on these two stools. But if they were not available, he would quickly claim two others. Pearl never argued with him.

"You know I love you. You're Daddy's special little girl. Do you want some Orange Crush or a milkshake? Nothing too good for my Pearl Girl."

November 3, 2021

Miriam Ross squinted while keeping her focus on making the left-hand turn onto Charlotte Street. A prolonged glance at a bright light could put her in the throes of a full-blown migraine, and she had no time for that. A blinding light had been bouncing off the back window of the car in front since turning off Sydney Street, and she'd missed her chance to squeeze into the left lane. With traffic this heavy there was no guarantee she'd be able to get over to go straight along Charlotte so she could turn left onto Princess, and she had no time for driving down King Street and circling onto Germain. Distraction had already put her dangerously close to being late.

Second appointments were always a good sign, and she was quite confident 197 Princess Street had checked all the boxes for the young couple she was meeting there today. Since starting with Remax she'd developed a pretty good instinct for serious buyers. Rachel and Justin Garrity were young professionals, with no children, no pets, a Mini Cooper, and a Jeep. The Garritys were currently renting on the east side, but were anxious to be uptown. Miriam figured they were looking to establish equity and spend a few years living in the city before making their next move. Making a good impression this time around might give her the sale when they were ready to trade city life for suburban life in the valley.

"Rachel grew up in Quispamsis, but her parents and two older siblings lived on Duke Street before she was born," Justin explained at the first viewing.

"They think we're crazy for buying in the south end, but I love the old buildings," Rachel added. "We've been in a box of an apartment on Hickey Road. I want a house with some character."

Miriam pulled up in front of the house. This was an excellent property. The present owners had decorated it in a way that enhanced the original woodwork and architecture while giving it a modern vibe. Two of the bedrooms had been converted into office spaces, leaving a good-sized spare bedroom and a luxurious primary bedroom. Four bedrooms offered wonderful resale value and a lot more space than the Garritys currently needed.

This house was one block from Justin's office, the Imperial Theatre, King's Square, and just a few blocks from Rachel's workplace. Right down Princess, a choice of the city's best restaurants and nightlife added to the attraction. The house showed well, and Miriam wasn't surprised to get the call back. The other contender had sold three days ago, which would probably add to the immediacy of the couple's decision.

Miriam did a quick check of her hair in the rear view. No time to apply fresh lipstick, as she could see the Garritys' Jeep pulling up behind her. She hated running late. She much preferred spending a few minutes inside the property, preparing her pitch, then meeting the clients at the door as if she were welcoming them to her home. Preparing, pitching, and pretending. Her three Ps were a winning formula, making her top saleswoman for two years in a row. The pretending made her reality more tolerable.

1958

Hank finished buttoning his father's white shirt and tucked it into his grey flannel pants. The shirt was a few sizes too big, but under his blue blazer, no one would notice. He grabbed the tie off the bed, looking quickly toward the street. He'd been sure George would come through for him, but no red Chevy had pulled up, and they'd be leaving for the church soon. Last night's call had been awkward, with Hank wishing he'd come clean on George's last visit. Of course, George had been shocked when Hank called asking him to be the best man at his wedding the next day.

"Jesus, man. What the hell? Give your head a shake. The last thing you need is a wife and a kid. Who you trying to fool?"

George didn't know shit. Hank had been just a dumb kid the first time they'd kissed. A friend should be the one standing beside him today, but what had made him think George would show up all happy and supportive? Hank pulled the knot tighter. He'd get his father to be his best man. This wedding was all his idea anyway.

"Step up and do right by that girl. You knock her up, you marry her. And what's so bad about ending up like your old man? Nothing wrong with being a longshoreman, either. No reason you can't take the opportunities this port city provides. I've done okay by you all, haven't I? You never wanted for anything. If you find the work too hard, your Uncle Roy would probably apprentice you in his plumbing shop. People will always shit, my boy."

November 3, 2021

Gloria Hamilton stood back to see if the pegboard was straight. Pretty hard for the paintings to hang straight if the hooks weren't level. Ted always told her she had a crooked eye and never let her hang anything on the walls in the house.

"You'd have the walls pockmarked with nail holes if I didn't stop you. Just because our son is a crack filler doesn't mean you can punch holes willy-nilly."

A pegboard display wall in her studio had been Ted's idea. The lockdown and COVID restrictions had made street traffic nonexistent, and if she was being realistic, crowds were never going to beat down her door to buy paintings. But the studio space on Germain Street had never been retail-motivated anyway.

Seven years ago, when she'd rented this small space, she had just given up her apartment on Princess Street after living a year separated from Ted. A grown woman running away from home had caused quite a disruption in the family and a buzz through her small community. But in a sudden flash she'd chosen to face a problem she'd been ignoring.

It was a decision Gloria didn't regret, as it brought healing and recovery to both her and Ted, and their marriage ended up being stronger for it. Ready to go back home but not wanting to leave the freedom and novelty of living uptown, she'd compromised by renting a studio space with a small kitchen attached so she could indulge herself in what she'd come to enjoy about living alone in the city and having a quiet place to create.

Gloria was now coming in to Saint John to paint four days a week, which to some would seem an extravagance, but to her was well worth the rent. Painting had become a second career after thirty years of teaching, and the time spent in the city a novelty after forty years of country living. In the city she felt the way she'd felt when she was eighteen years old in her first apartment on Duke Street. *Sixty-eight is the new what?* Gloria chuckled to herself as she climbed up the stepstool to hang a print on the hooks at the top of the pegboard.

1958

Hank rolled over and looked at the clock radio. In two hours the alarm would go off and he'd drag himself out of bed, his father's voice echoing in his head.

"Get your sorry arse down to the docks before first light. Bed Bug Walton will get you on a gang if you show up early and work hard. For goodness' sake, boy, don't let it be said that Lucky Lowman's kid's a pansy and don't know how to work."

Hank considered getting up now so his tossing and turning didn't wake Tanya. She was so uncomfortable in the last weeks of her pregnancy. Hank had offered to sleep on the couch last night so as not to disturb her.

"Is it so bad that I want my husband to sleep beside me and show me a bit of affection?" Tanya had said when they'd gotten into bed last night. "I know I'm huge, but I won't break if you hug me."

"I'm tired, Tanya. I spent the whole day slinging two-hundred-pound bags of flour."

Most nights started out the same. Tanya wanted sex and he made some excuse to get out of it.

Hank reached over and turned off the alarm. He wasn't getting back to sleep, so he may as well get up and make his lunch.

What the hell were you thinking?

His father's voice was not the only one echoing in his head. George's words came to him several times a day.

1959

Tanya woke Hank around four in the morning on January 2. He called a Diamond taxi to take them to the General. As the car made its way across the viaduct, Hank caught sight of the lighted dome atop the hospital and recalled visiting George when he had his tonsils removed. He'd walked clear over from the north end with a tub of Baxter's ice cream in a paper bag, not even considering it would be liquid by the time he got it to his friend. A tonsillectomy, his mother assured him, was not life-threatening surgery, but until he saw George sitting up in his hospital bed, he had himself convinced his friend would not leave that frightening building alive.

In admitting they put Tanya right into a wheelchair and onto the elevator, leaving Hank dazed and confused, standing there like an idiot. Finally, some guy told him what floor the maternity ward was on. Once there, he sat down beside some other guy who looked as nervous as he felt.

"First baby?"

"Yeah."

"You'll probably be sitting here for a long time then. This is our fifth, and the last one came quick. It doesn't get any easier though. The women do all the work while we sit out here feeling helpless and stupid. Told the missus to get her tubes tied while she's here this time, but being a good Catholic, she won't hear of it."

Hank didn't know much about good Catholics, but the good Pentecostals were something he'd gotten to know about in the last few months. The Bennetts seemed friendly enough at first. Mrs. Bennett went out of her way to make sure the young man her daughter invited to church and brought home for dinner was well fed that day. She was cutting him a second piece of lemon meringue pie when Tanya blurted out that she was pregnant. Hank hadn't gotten his pie.

What followed was a bit of a blur, but both families had quickly joined forces to make sure the "kids" faced up to the responsibility of their mistake. The wedding took place right away, before Tanya's condition became obvious. The newlyweds moved into the Bennetts' basement. Tanya didn't go back to school, but Hank finished the year, then started at the port the day after graduation.

"Mr. Lowman. You have a baby girl. Your wife was a trooper."

Hank felt nauseous and weak as he got to his feet. A baby girl. A baby. He had a baby. He was a father. He was eighteen. This hadn't been how he'd seen his future. He had dreams, dreams of leaving Saint John, dreams of becoming what he'd thought about for as long as he could remember.

They had begun the day Hank ripped the cellophane off the first album he'd bought with his own money at the Woolworths. Putting the vinyl record on the turntable was life changing, and it wasn't until years later he realized not everyone listened to music the same way he did. He didn't know then that being a sound engineer was even a job, but reading album notes he memorized anything associated with sound and slowly started discovering everything he could about the art of mixing and engineering vocals and instruments.

"Are you all right, Mr. Lowman? You can go in and see your wife and meet your little girl."

November 3, 2021

*L*iam Matthews passed a hard copy of his resume to the managing director sitting across the desk from him. He'd considered emailing it to Scott Mercer, but decided at the last minute to take a chance and drive in. Masking in public places was now mandatory, but at least the lockdown was over. When he and Amanda had filled the U-Haul and headed east, they'd had no idea what was ahead. In February 2020, nobody did, even though the daily news coming from places like Italy and China was alarming. At least they'd gotten to New Brunswick before travelling from province to province became complicated.

Throwing a pregnancy into the move made it even more challenging. Being near family was the main reason for moving back, and the support they'd received since the baby's birth validated that decision. But lately, Liam had begun to wonder if, in moving home, he'd sacrificed the career he'd worked so hard to establish. A job at the Imperial would quiet some of the angst he felt about that, even if what they were offering right now was just part-time.

As a kid Liam had been completely enthralled with the Imperial Theatre. He remembered sitting in the balcony listening to Murray McLauchlin in 1995. The lights and sound brought the theatre alive, and Liam had felt the thrill of that to his core. Tears ran down his cheeks at one point during that concert, but he'd quickly swiped them away, not wanting his dad and older brother to see how emotional the night was for him.

Liam's father had parked a few blocks away, and walking into King's Square had been another highlight of the night. The X-shaped walkways of the square led to the elaborate bandstand twinkling with what seemed like thousands of lights. Concertgoers and patrons of the Paramount taking in the opening night of *Legends of the Fall* filled the pathways, and the bustle filled his ears while his gaze swivelled between the two marquees opposite each other, Woolworths and Diana Restaurant signs and the looming Saint John City Market lit up against the dark sky adding to the magic and novelty of the night. Saint John was the big city to an eleven-year-old country boy.

"You certainly are qualified, Liam," said Scott now, "and I have no reservations about offering you the job. My only regret is that it isn't full-time employment. With this whole pandemic mess, it's a wonder we're still open at all." He got up and walked over to a photograph on the wall. "I was here the day they cut the ribbon for the official grand opening in 1994."

"It's an amazing venue, that's for sure. I came to my first concert here in 1995," Liam said.

"The only reason this theatre exists in its present glory is because of a massive amount of vision and dedication of a few people in this city," Scott continued, pointing to another framed photograph. "They gave the Full Gospel Assembly a one-dollar down payment with the promise of another $999,999 payment in one year, and they made good on their promise. Bringing the theatre back to its original 1913 grandeur took eleven years."

"Wow, that's impressive," Liam said.

"It sure is," Scott said. "And I don't want to be the one to let it go under just because we can't fill the seats right now. We'll do what we can and hope for brighter days ahead. The show must go on, and we can't do that without a professional sound and lighting team. We'd be happy to have you join that team if you can temporarily get by with only part-time hours."

A few minutes later Liam found himself sitting on a bench in King's Square, staring up at the marquee across the street. Tears, like at the concert so long ago, were close to the surface, and if he let it, the emotion would overtake him. He was home, living a ferry crossing away from the house he'd grown up in and a quick drive from the theatre he'd dreamt about working in for such a long time. In three days, he'd take his place on the team that would bring every act and event to life on the stage of the historic theatre.

A swoop of pigeons brought him quickly out of his emotional trance. He watched as the birds landed very near his feet and began pecking at the ground and at each other. Turning his head, he scanned the people milling about. There was a mix—teenagers fooling around, the F-word punctuating every interaction; a couple of older women, one dragging a suitcase on wheels; and a circle of old men no doubt tackling all the troubles of the world.

Probably most of the people in the mix had things pretty tough, a lot tougher than he did. He had Amanda, a new baby girl, a house to live in, food in his cupboards and fridge, a beat-up VW that was still going strong, and parents who would always help him in any way they could. And now he had a job at the Imperial Theatre.

"She's a beauty, isn't she?"

It took Liam a second or two to realize the man who'd just sat down at the other end of the bench was speaking to him, and that he was referring to the theatre across the street.

"Yes, she sure is."

"They called her the Capitol when I was a kid. I saw some good films there back in the day. Not silent ones, although I probably look that old to you. Every Saturday they had a matinee. Lots of westerns. Roy Rogers was my favorite."

"Trigger was his horse, right?"

"Now, you're too young to remember that."

"We had horses next door when I was growing up, and my dad always called one of them Trigger. He grew up in Britain, but apparently they watched Roy Rogers over there too."

"Growing up here I never imagined travelling anywhere, but ended up in California. No one's travelling much these days with that damn virus going on. Small world, really, when you think about it. My grandmother came from England. A war bride. 'Folks are more alike than different,' she used to say, and as a kid I had no clue what that meant. I kind of get it now."

::

Hank kept his eye focused on the marquee announcing the upcoming Blue Rodeo concert while the young man's exuberance for the job he'd just landed at the Imperial provided the rest of the conversation. If Hank started talking about training in San Francisco and then recording and mixing the albums of most of the well-known artists in the sixties and seventies, it would just seem like a tall tale coming from a scruffy old man in rags. Listing the bands, artists, and albums he'd had a part in producing would only impress this young fellow, if he believed a word of it.

Hank stood and steadied himself on the arm of the bench. "Have a good day, young fella."

1960

Hank pulled open the heavy door. Entering this building always felt foreboding and somewhat suffocating. Making his way down the narrow hall to Gran's room, he knew the woman he was visiting was not the grandmother he longed to talk to, but leaving without saying goodbye to her would make it even harder.

Gran had come to the TB hospital six months ago, and it seemed this was to be her final dwelling. She still knew everyone but seemed to see them in the framework of whatever decade she found herself in at the time. She seemed unaware of her present surroundings and was often back on Ludlow Street as a young bride, a busy mother raising nine children, or a lonely widow. Sometimes she travelled even further afield and would be walking the cobbled streets of her village in the Cotswolds as a child or a young woman working in the scullery of the Broadway Hotel. It was astounding how quickly she could transport through time and place.

"Henry, God love you. I'm so glad you stopped by. You've got to tell your grandfather to call Spragg's and arrange a delivery. I'd call him myself but the bloke won't come on my bidding. Damn fool thinks a woman can't know when the coal is running out. 'You'll need your husband to call,' he said last time I rang him. The cold weather's upon us, lad, and the coal bin is nearly empty."

There was no point telling Gran that Granddad had been dead ten years and the coal stove was removed the summer after he died. Instead, Hank asked how much she needed and what day would be good for delivery.

"How was school? You're a smart lad and the spit of my brother Thomas. The spit of him."

Hank moved his chair closer, hoping that maybe if she saw the stubble on his cheek, she'd realize he was a grown man. He pulled the afghan up tighter around her shoulders.

"Are you warm enough, Gran?"

"I'm fine. Can't sit here much longer, though. The boys will be in soon and supper needs fixing. Gerald is always famished when he comes through the door. I'd fancy a cuppa builder's first though."

"I'm sure they'll be along with tea soon."

"Do you figure I'm the queen or something, having someone bring me my tea? I can fix my own cuppa."

"Gran. I have something to tell you."

"Well then tell it, lad. You can't sit still, can ya? Just like my brother Randall. He was the worst for staying put. Had twenty houses to my one, I'm sure of it. Couldn't settle, that boy."

"I'm leaving Saint John for a bit, Gran. I need to go."

"Well, if you need to, then I reckon there's no stopping ya. Mother used to say the only thing to keep Randall home would be a yoke and chain. Where you gallivanting off to?"

"I'm going to California."

"Going to be a movie star, are you, lad?"

Hank let the question hang in the air. Was Gran really taking in what he was saying or was she playing along with what she thought were the imaginings of a young boy? Hank stood to take his wallet from his back pocket. He opened it and pulled out a photograph.

"This was Jennifer Dawn's first birthday. She sure loved her cake, as you can tell from how much frosting is on her little face."

"Well, she's a darling. And whose baby is she?"

"She's mine, Gran."

"Well, isn't that brilliant, and you just out of nappies yourself. God love her little soul."

::

Hank stepped out the door into the bitter cold. He'd walk across the causeway and catch a bus to the north end at King's Square. The walk might clear his head. Last night's fight had been a bad one. The screaming woke Jennifer up. Tanya hurled her angry accusation at him before going into their bedroom and slamming the door behind her. Hank got Jennifer out of her crib.

"Is it me you hate or is it just that I'm not George? This act you're putting on isn't fooling anyone. Don't be such a fucking coward and admit it."

Hank had rocked Jennifer back to sleep with tears streaming down his cheeks. Now, with the wind off Courtney Bay whipping his face, he allowed the tears to fall again. He would find the courage to follow through. Tomorrow morning, he would get on that bus.

1960

At the bottom of King Street, Hank hoisted his duffel bag onto his other shoulder. The SMT bus was leaving early, too early to have caught a bus over from Lansdowne, so he'd walked the whole way. Leaving while everyone slept was better anyway. He had no intention of telling anyone he was leaving. Going to tell Gran yesterday had been hard enough, and she had no idea what was really happening. She thought him a schoolboy with a big dream and no responsibilities.

He had been trying for months to ignore how he was feeling. He got up and went to work every day and felt some pride in being able to hand his pay envelope over to Tanya every week. He loved the way it felt to have Jennifer's little arms around his neck and feel her tiny kisses on his cheek. If only he felt something when Tanya kissed him or snuggled into him at night.

Hank choked back emotion as he thought back to the beginning of their last fight.

"Am I so disgusting you can't even touch me?" Tanya cried. "We haven't had sex for months. Why the hell did you marry me if you don't love me?"

Did he love her? Had he ever? They only dated for four months and had only had sex twice when she'd told him she was pregnant, making him wonder if it was even his. He'd actually hoped she'd admit to having been with some other guy so he could break up with her. But she said he'd been the only one, so he did the right thing.

With him gone, Tanya could do better. There were a lot of guys who'd be more than willing to take his place. And he was confident Tanya's parents would make sure she and Jennifer were provided for. They'd step up and pay the rent on the apartment or let Tanya move back into their basement. Tanya would find someone else, and Jennifer would soon forget who he was.

None of that changed the fact that he was running out on his wife and daughter or lessened the knowledge of how disappointed his parents would be in him.

For months thoughts of leaving were constant, waking him in the night and clutching at his insides during the daytime. He'd felt such relief buying the bus ticket yesterday, knowing he'd sneak out in the early morning without a word. He knew how ridiculous it would have sounded if he'd told anyone he was catching the seven thirty bus and going to California. The bus only went as far as Calais.

November 5, 2021

O n the day of the eviction, Hank had stood on the sidewalk beside Eddie Winchester long after the rest of the guys had left. Eddie had only been in the rooming house for a few months but of all the other residents Hank was going to miss Eddie the most. Watching as the last items were thrown in the dumpster, a light rain started to fall.

"Well, ain't this a kick in the pants?" Eddie had said. "It's been a while since I had to plunk my old carcass on a cot in a shelter, but I don't see that I've got a whole lot of other options. What about you?"

"I've never had to sleep in a shelter. I stayed at the Salvation Army hostel before moving in here, but they closed that down. I don't have a clue where to go."

"Do you have any family in town?" Eddie asked.

"No," Hank answered. "What about you?"

"None that want anything to do with me," Eddie answered.

::

Hank had gone with Eddie to the Outflow shelter feeling somewhat nervous and vulnerable. For the last seven years he'd had his own room in a well-secured building. The first few nights at the shelter hadn't been too bad, and having Eddie there had helped. But Eddie had been wrong about his family not wanting anything to do with him. He'd called a sister and she had offered to let him stay at her house in Sussex. She'd picked Eddie up yesterday and left Hank feeling like a kid on the playground with no friends.

Tonight, he settled in to a restless sleep only to be woken soon after by a voice with a cadence so familiar he'd felt a jolt of joy as he opened his eyes. The voice was coming from the tall figure a few feet away. It wasn't

Marvin, of course, but taking in the bright ensemble, the sequins and bling, Hank smiled. Marvin would have loved the person's fashion choices.

Hank laid back down, pulling the blankets over his face again. He brought his hands up to cover his ears, hoping to mute the similar-sounding voice and quiet the memories. Then an angry tirade took over; the tone and message of the last words were just as familiar and heartbreaking.

"Pick a gender, you faggot."

Within a few short minutes he'd felt both elation and terror, and as Hank squeezed his eyes shut, he knew that tomorrow night he would find a different place to sleep.

1960

Hank peered out the grimy window of the phone booth, keeping his eye on the bus. The driver had announced a fifteen-minute break before crossing the border. He could probably have waited and tried to call George from the US side, but he wasn't sure the pay phones would take Canadian coins. He was so unsure of everything and had pretty much been trembling with fear since the bus pulled away from King Street. The nervousness he'd felt sneaking around silently in the dark, not wanting to wake Tanya or the baby, had changed to exhilaration when he'd stepped out onto the quiet early morning sidewalk. But it quickly became fright and second-guessing after boarding the bus.

He'd thought about calling George last night but had been afraid someone would overhear the conversation. He couldn't leave without saying goodbye. Funny how leaving his wife and child and his parents without a word was okay, but he felt the need to tell George what he was doing. He would understand; he knew what Hank's dreams had always been. George knew Hank better than anyone, maybe even better than Hank knew himself.

It was two months after the wedding when George showed up in Saint John. There hadn't been a phone call or anything acknowledging the marriage or explaining why he hadn't come to be Hanks's best man. Hank happened to be visiting his parents when he saw George's car drive up. He finished his meal trying to calm himself and act as if everything was fine.

After supper Hank went out to the stoop and lit a cigarette, waiting for George to join him. It was George's fault he smoked. The way George rolled up his pack of Export A in his T-shirt sleeve was the coolest James Dean kind of thing and Hank soon did the same. Growing up, Hank thought everything George did was cool.

The conversation had been pretty much what Hank expected, with a few more swear words thrown in. George let his disapproval rip and Hank didn't counter it with much of anything. What argument could he make, knowing that marrying Tanya was probably the biggest mistake of his life since the day he'd said yes to the damn Sadie Hawkins dance invitation? He knew no justification would cut it with George.

George would understand this, though. He would give Hank the encouragement and understanding he needed to get himself back on that bus and keep going. Hank dropped the quarter in the slot and dialled the number, his anxiety increasing with each ring. Maybe George was sleeping or outside.

Hank could see some of the other passengers making their way across the parking lot toward the bus. He hadn't noticed the driver returning yet though. He would let the phone ring a few more times.

"Hello?"

"Hello."

"Yeah, that's what I said." George seemed out of breath; his voice annoyed.

"It's me." Hank said.

"Yeah."

"I only have a couple of minutes. I've got to get back on the bus."

"What bus?"

"I left. I'm finally doing it."

"Doing what? If you've only got a couple of minutes, spit it out, don't talk in riddles. Where the hell are you?"

"I'm in St. Stephen. I'm heading to California. I'm doing what I always said I would do."

"Well, holy shit. Good for you, Hanky-Pank."

Hank felt his heart lurch at the old nickname. "I couldn't leave without saying goodbye. I'm sorry we fell out."

"We didn't fall out, Hank. You knocked a girl up, married her, and became a daddy. Where the hell did I fit into that? Figured staying down here was the best thing for both of us."

"You still fishing?"

"Yeah. I never had any grand career plans like you did. I just like keeping busy and working hard. Being out on choppy water and pulling lobster traps fifteen hours a day, don't give me a lot of time to feel sorry for myself. I'm proud of you, Hanky-Pank. I always knew you'd make something of yourself."

"Got to go," Hank said, his heart racing. The unspoken words beat in Hank's chest and the silence on the other end seemed deafening. He turned his head and saw the driver boarding the bus, but Hank felt frozen in the moment.

"You take care of yourself," George said. "Don't go getting yourself killed or anything stupid. Just do what you've always dreamt of and be who you're supposed to be. Fuck the rest of it."

"Bye, George."

"Adios, shithead. Just take care of yourself."

"I'm sorry."

"Yeah, whatever. Go catch your bus."

Hank kept the receiver to his ear while reaching for his bag. He did not want their last conversation to end this way.

"I love you," said Hank, the whispered words stuck in his throat. His shaking hands replaced the receiver before he bolted from the phone booth.

Hank ran across the parking lot, swiping at the stupid tears running down his face.

November 6, 2021

H ank did not consider himself a thief, but stealing a shopping cart from the parking lot of the Giant Tiger hurt no one and was certainly making it much easier to haul around his few possessions and the blankets and the sleeping bag the shelter had given him. And walking by a building site on Waterloo, he'd noticed what seemed to be a perfectly good tarp lying in a heap. The workmen hadn't valued it enough to fold it up and take it with them, but Hank realized how valuable this sturdy tarp could be. He folded it up as best he could and laid it in the cart. He then picked up several large spikes, a good-sized rock, and three cement blocks.

He'd been relieved to see the cart and its contents untouched when he came out of Stone Church a few minutes ago. The hot meal had satisfied the gnawing hunger which seemed to be his normal state, and he'd stayed inside the warm building as long as he could. He then walked around a bit, having no intention of sleeping in the shelter again. The hatred in those angry words felt way too familiar, and he couldn't bring himself to risk hearing them again. He would find an empty bench in King's Square.

Hank pushed the rickety shopping cart into the square. He laid out on the bench facing the Imperial and covered up, hoping to get a few hours of uninterrupted sleep. As quiet as the Square might be at midnight, Hank knew just how quickly things could change. He had kept a wide berth from the violence he'd heard earlier going on across the street in the Loyalist Graveyard. The uproar had culminated with several police cars and an ambulance roaring up Sydney Street.

He was too old to fight for his security every night. Tomorrow he'd find an out-of-the-way place and put today's finds to use.

1960

arvin Corbett hung the heavy coat on the rack, taking a few minutes to catch his breath. Costume changes were hard at the best of times, but going from a wool overcoat to a pink ball gown at least gave him a chance to cool down and get his wits about him. Costume changes and gender confusion were nothing new to him.

He would have made such a beautiful little girl. The first time Grammie said this, his father had spat out venomous words peppered with hatred and disgust, tempering any excitement Marvin felt with the arrival of his beloved grandmother.

"Language, Robert," she'd said. "Your Uncle Joseph had feminine features and he fathered fourteen children." Feminine features had helped Marvin land this role; no one could pull off a ball gown and heels like Marvin Corbett.

The family had tolerated long lashes, pastel clothing, and girly interests, but full-blown homosexuality was not something Marvin's parents, siblings, aunts, uncles, or the Corbetts' church family could stomach, so Grammie had suggested he broaden his horizons.

"He's not going to have an acting career in Florenceville, New Brunswick," Grammie told everyone the summer he left home. "Our Marvin is going to make a name for himself someday."

No name in lights on the off-Broadway marquee, but the playbill said *Transvestite No. 2: Marvin Corbett*, and for now that was good enough.

"Zip me up," Marvin bellowed.

November 7, 2021

Pearl stepped back as if trying to get away from her own shrill voice and angry words. When she found herself having one of these tirades, all she heard was her mother's voice. Sometimes she'd be mid-sentence and have no idea what she was even angry about. But backing down seemed impossible right now, unless she just walked away and went into her building.

"She's crazy."

Pearl watched two women quickly cross the street rather than walk into the middle of the altercation.

"The apple didn't fall far from the tree," her father had always said—and if that was the case, maybe she was crazy.

"And if you think you can...this is just bullshit."

Pearl pulled her fleece jacket tighter and fumbled with the zipper. Maybe it was the bite in the air putting her in such a foul mood, causing her to pick a fight with this man. Spending lots of time outside was how she'd gotten through the last several months, but it was getting harder now that the air was colder, and a November snow turning to rain had covered the sidewalks with ice. Seasonal Affective Disorder, the shrink called it. "Christ, that's all I need," had been her reply. As if forty years in an alcoholic stupor hadn't been enough.

Her sobriety had been hard won, and she hadn't taken a drink in seven years. Looking in the mirror every morning, she marvelled at the improvement recovery had brought. But she knew that to others she was the black-haired, balding, creepy old woman who walked the city streets all hours of the day as if she were a ghost looking for her rightful home.

Crazy and probably drunk was how she figured most folks saw her, even if they'd never heard her lose her shit at random strangers. The man she'd taken a strip off a few minutes ago had just driven away, leaving her to decide if she'd keep walking or retreat inside to calm down. People seldom spoke or made eye contact, which was probably for the best.

But why would strangers be any different than her own children? "Unpredictable," David always said. "A nutbar," was Kenny's description. "A basket case," Ruth called her. She never tried to convince them otherwise, even after she stopped drinking. She'd fired the same judgement at her own mother and completely understood the embarrassment her children felt. They had their own lives to live, and she would carry on living hers as best she could.

At least she could still afford her small apartment, and she didn't need much. Surprising how few groceries one frail old women needs. Whatever she had was a hell of a lot better than ending up where her poor old mother did. Not that CentraCare was there anymore.

Pearl had walked all the way to the west side one day to sit in the grassy area where the old brick buildings had stood. Sitting on the bench, the mist and stench of the roiling falls in her nostrils, she'd sobbed for her dead mother. Maybe someday her own children would do the same, wherever they decided her shrine should be.

1960

The first night Hank hadn't noticed how shabby the rooming house was or the putrid stench in the stairwell. The next night it hit him, but he plugged his nose, closed the door behind him, and felt grateful for the narrow cot and the silence. Now, three weeks later he was resigned to the dreary accommodations and the gruelling routine. After fifteen hours working through sleet and chilling winds, he was happy to flop down on the hard mattress and pull the scratchy blanket up over his shoulders.

He'd gotten off the bus in Calais knowing he'd have to work his way west. The two hundred dollars he'd managed to bring with him wouldn't get him very far. A guy on the bus told him a huge road building project was underway in Maine, offering plenty of labourer jobs that paid workers under the table. Hank knew those were the only kind of jobs he'd be able to land as a Canadian citizen.

"Get up, Lowman. The truck leaves in forty minutes."

Hank jumped off his cot and grabbed his boots. As he did most nights, he'd slept in his clothes, giving him enough time to run to the diner and scoff some breakfast down. The days he'd tried to work on an empty stomach hadn't gone so well. The food truck on site charged a fortune for stale sandwiches and disgusting coffee.

Getting into the back of the truck, Hank could hear the opening lines of "Heartbreak Hotel." Did Tanya think of him when she heard Elvis belt out those lines about being left? Did she have any idea why he left, or what he was heading toward? He heard the mix, bass, pitch, and timbre, not just the lyrics. He knew working these long days were going to get him closer to California and closer to the day he'd get to sit at a mixing board. Someday he'd listen to a song on the radio and know he'd had a part in making it happen. Someday people would read his name on album jackets.

November 7, 2021

Waiting for the pedestrian walk light, Hank gazed over at the fenced-in crater on the corner where Woolworths used to be. Both corners looked so different from how he remembered them when he was a kid. King Street was bustling, a shopping centre for most folks, with Woolworths as the main attraction. Across the square the Dominion store had been the only place his mother would go for groceries. She always counted on Clifford Ashe to cut and wrap her meat. Restaurants had come and gone: the Riviera, Greens, Venus, Diana, and Olympia. And so had theatres: the Capitol, the Strand, the Paramount within sight of the city square, and the Kent a block away.

So many memories a stone's throw from where Hank was standing and where he now spent most of his long days before returning to his makeshift shelter for the night. He recalled the day he'd stuffed his duffel bag in the luggage compartment of the SMT bus parked halfway down this hill. He'd looked around to see if anyone had noticed Gerard and Annette Lowman's boy getting on a bus headed for the United States.

It took five months to get up enough nerve to call home. His mother had answered the telephone and before saying anything else told him his disappearance had killed his grandmother.

"Such a disgrace to have a grandson who just up and leaves his wife and child."

Hank didn't bother to argue that Gran wouldn't have been disgraced unless someone told her she should be. He was still a little boy to her, and she could have been told anything to explain his absence, if she even noticed it. The shame of him leaving hadn't killed his grandmother, but his mother's words hit him hard.

"Just wanted you to know I was alive, Mom."

1960

The money Hank earned in Maine got him as far as Indianapolis, Indiana, with a few dollars to spare. After hitchhiking to the town of Stroh, he'd landed a job with a guy hiring a crew to go farm to farm harvesting the corn crop. Men followed the machines that cut down the corn, gathering the stalks and binding them into sheaves. After tying the sheaves they'd stack them in bunches throughout the field. Then each stook would be loaded onto a trailer and unloaded into the barns to be dried. When they finished on one farm, they'd move on to another, pitching tents along the way.

Bringing in the sheaves, bringing in the sheaves. Tramping through the field, Hank could hear his Nanny Dickson's shrill voice belting out that hymn at Main Street Baptist as he stood beside her, trying not to laugh at the comical sight of the organ player's huge rear end swallowing the piano stool. Going to the Church of England with Gran was never as entertaining.

The days were long and Hank was bone tired when he bedded down at night, but thoughts of California got him back up to start all over in the morning. Harvesting would be steady work but short term. He'd save every possible cent so when the work was over, he could move on. Luckily most farms they worked fed the crew at least one good meal a day, which Hank decided right away would have to do. The more money he saved, the further he could go the next time he hopped a bus.

"Lowman, you sure you won't come into town with us? You might get lucky at the bar tonight. Rodney says the ladies are all over us travelling farm boys."

"No, I'll pass."

"You got a lady back home, boy?"

"No."

"Not a real talker, are ya? Where is home, anyway? Can't quite figure that twang of yours out. You from Maine?"

"Canada, actually."

"You don't say. What the hell you doing stacking corn in the heartland of the USA?"

"I'm working my way west."

"Going to be a movie star, are ya?"

"I need to take a piss," Hank said, walking away.

November 8, 2021

Bruce Smith rolled the trolley of new garbage cans along the paved walkway of the Loyalist Burial Ground. In his forty-three years working for the City of Saint John he'd never seen the amount of vandalism and disregard for public spaces he was now seeing every day. It was taking the fun out of the job. Some might think his job menial and unimportant, but he'd always taken pride in keeping the city looking nice. Forty-six years of doing just that while trying to make a living and provide for his family. For a high school dropout, steady work, a decent wage, benefits, and a pension plan had been nothing to scoff at.

With retirement approaching, Bruce should be looking forward to a life of leisure, but with Edna getting half his pension in the divorce settlement, he knew he'd have to find work elsewhere to make ends meet. He was just making rent on his one-bedroom Orange Street apartment as it was. He'd stay working if it were up to him, but management thought a sixty-four-year-old man wasn't up to the physical demands of this job, even though he still carried his weight and worked twice as hard as the younger guys. Good Old Smitty, they all called him, and usually he was the guy with all the jokes, good humour, and can-do spirit. Lately, though, it had been hard keeping up that façade.

"New garbage cans, eh?"

Bruce turned toward the voice. Even though the man walking toward him had his hood pulled up and tied tightly, Bruce could see the wrinkled, whiskered face and guessed he was probably several years older than himself. A sparkle in the man's deep blue eyes emitted some vulnerability as well as kindness, and Bruce felt no threat.

"Yes. Maybe they'll leave these alone for a bit," Bruce answered. "In what world does it make sense to start a barrel fire in a plastic garbage can?"

"Better than having a bonfire in the middle of the bandstand across the street, though, don't you think? The poor buggers are just trying to keep warm."

"Well, I guess you're right. Keeps us busy, I'll tell you."

"Too bad the folks who pay your salary don't see how desperately this city needs more low-income housing."

"That's true. I'm Bruce, by the way, but most folks call me Smitty. What's your name?"

"Hank. Sorry if I sound pissed off, but it's real hard to find a decent place to live right now. The rooming house I was in for the last seven years just got bought by some property developer, which put a lot of old guys like me out on the street. They're turning it into high-end apartments, which won't be affordable for the average person. When I was growing up in this city, a person could afford to buy a decent house. Doesn't seem to be that way now, even for those earning a good wage. So, what the hell is an old codger like me supposed to do?"

"I hear what you're saying. The wife and I bought one of those wartime houses over North in 1981 for $68,000. We thought that was a lot back then, but I'd just gotten on permanent with the city and Edna was a nurse, so we managed the mortgage payments and some renovations. The price it sold for last year was unbelievable. You'd think I'd be rolling in dough, but divorce is a costly business."

"Nothing easy about any of it. Then throw a damn pandemic into the works."

Bruce put the last garbage can in place and started pulling the trolley back toward the truck parked beside the curb. "Nice to meet you, Hank. Hope things start looking up for you."

Bruce lifted the trolley onto the back of the truck. Meeting Hank had been enough to put an end to the pity party he'd been having this morning. It didn't seem as if the old guy had found another place to live after being evicted. He was probably living on the street, which was so much worse than anything Bruce was facing. Sure, he regretted not trying harder to fix things when his marriage fell apart, and of course he wished he'd been a better husband and father. He also wished Donald and Patti came around more and that they let him see the grandkids more than a couple times a year.

Bruce jumped into the driver's seat and pulled away from the curb. Good Old Smitty would keep smiling, making the guys laugh, and doing what he did best. He'd give his all to the city for the next five months and fifteen days and accept his retirement with pride. He'd worry about what would come next the day after.

1961

*L*eaving through the main entrance of the Los Angeles Greyhound Bus depot, Hank felt the heat hit him. The driver said the sweltering temperature was normal for July in California, but Hank hadn't felt anything like it before. From the bus windows he'd seen the stream of traffic, both cars and pedestrians, on the Los Angeles streets, but the bumper-to-bumper vehicles racing down East 6th Street had him in a trance. Standing stupidly, his mouth open and eyes transfixed in a stare, Hank was jostled by the rush of bodies on the sidewalk.

Harvest wages had been good up until early November, then Hank had taken a job on a farm helping the farmer finish up the construction of a large barn, and stayed to work all winter with room and board thrown in. He'd been hired on at several farms in the spring, helping with the planting. By then he'd saved quite a wad of cash and was able to pay the fare to take the Greyhound bus almost three thousand miles, with enough left over to live on until he got work in LA.

The first thing Hank would have to do was apply for a green card. Working under the table was not an option long term if he was going to get work that could pay the cost of living in this city and let him save for the day he could enroll in the sound engineering program in San Francisco.

November 9, 2021

W alking up to the door on Duke Street, not much looked different from the day he'd left. The dumpster was still there, and it looked like a new front door had been installed. There was a security panel requiring a code to enter.

Hank had hoped to at least get into the building to look for his October Old Age cheque. He hadn't even thought of it until this morning. His small monthly pension from United Western was deposited into his bank account, but the government cheque came in the mail. Hopefully he could find October's and figure out how he'd get November's. Were the mail slots still mounted on the wall inside the front door? Was any of the previous residents' mail still there? Hank stood awkwardly on the sidewalk. A van with a construction company logo was parked in the driveway.

Hank stepped up to the door and knocked loudly. A few seconds later the door opened and two men toting buckets of crack-filling compound walked out. Hank held the door open, then squeezed by them without a word. The mail cubicles were gone, as was the wainscoting and dingy wallpaper that had covered the vestibule walls. A pile of garbage had been swept into the corner and Hank spotted a few envelopes mixed in with discarded strips of wallpaper. As Hank pawed through the pile, he could feel anger rising in his chest. Twelve men had lived at this address, and it was unlikely that any of them had found a new residence, let alone filled out change-of-address forms. No one had bothered to show them respect enough to put a plan in place so that they'd receive the government cheques they counted on to survive.

Hank pulled out any brown envelopes he saw, knowing the likelihood of finding most of the displaced men they were addressed to was slim. He knew an address to send Eddie's if he found it and he had run into a couple of the other guys at Stone Church or at the Outflow coffee truck. Better chance of them getting their cheques if he took them than if they were scooped up and thrown in the dumpster outside.

1961

Marvin stood on the sidewalk in front of the Caffe Cino. The exterior looked untouched, but several barricades prevented entry. An early morning fire had gutted the interior. *Go west, young man* was a mantra Marvin had been hearing more and more, and he had started giving it some thought. This theatre had given him a purpose, a place to belong, and without that, moving on might be the best alternative.

"Move, faggot," hollered a man as he bumped Marvin out of the way.

Daytime hostility and nighttime terror were nothing new, but maybe it was time to leave New York and head for California. The Caffe Cino was home, the theatre his life, and with it gone there was nothing keeping him in New York.

"Take these pearls, my love, and you'll always have a part of your old grandmother with you. They look more beautiful on you than they ever did on me. You are who you are, my dear Marvin, and God loves you just as you are."

Marvin reached up to touch Grammie Corbett's pearls, part of every ensemble he wore. He had almost left them in the dressing room last night, and at the last moment realized they were on his dressing table, not around his neck. But he had lost the mink stole Grammie had given him. When he wrapped that tattered mink stole around his neck, he still smelled his Grammie and felt her love. Grammie, the only one in his big Baptist family who really saw him and loved him anyway.

November 9, 2021

*G*loria watched as the postal employee opened the mail slot. It was only
flyers, most likely, as very little came to this address. She had changed
a few things to the Princess Street address the year she'd lived there but
had changed everything back to the farm address when she moved back
home. Only the Saint John Energy bill and bank correspondence regarding
the separate studio account she kept at CIBC came to this Germain Street
address. Lots of flyers and advertising, though. She kept them in a box by
the front door, and when the box was full took it home for Ted to start the
furnace with.

Gloria still remembered the small apartment she'd rented on Princess
eight years ago with fondness. It had been such a cozy little space, filled
with only things she loved and needed, a far cry from the huge house
she'd raised four kids in and maintained since she and Ted built it in the
mid-eighties. It was so nice having a space that was just hers. The small
studio apartment had been perfect for her at the time and she'd loved
every square inch of it.

She had also loved the exercise of looking after herself and letting
all the other grown people in her life do the same. And Ted had rallied to
do just that after the initial shock wore off. It had been an awakening for
them both, and not a day went by when Gloria wasn't thankful that she'd
listened to her inner voice and left, forcing them both to work on themselves and on their marriage.

Oh, how quickly a year goes by. She had signed a year's lease in July
2013 with the intention of being alone and watching four seasons from
the five windows looking out onto Princess and Sydney Streets. She needed to have the clear periphery of twelve months in which to focus on her
recovery and rediscovery. She strongly believed Ted needed that too, although he'd shown a lot of resistance at first.

And here it was, almost the end of another year. November already. There had been ice on her windshield this morning and Ted had suggested she wait until later to go into the city, but she'd scraped off her windshield and headed in eagerly. Christmas orders kept her busy and motivated, but the real reason she valued her studio days so much was that coming here gave her the same good feelings she'd felt during her year on Princess when she was doing something just for herself. Of course, she was happy to be a wife, a mother, a grandmother, a sister-in-law, a friend, and a member of her community, but while being all that, she would make sure she had something just for herself. She had long ago given up feeling selfish for it.

1961

"*C*an you lift a shovel?"

"Well, yeah," Hank replied.

"Then you've got a job if you show up here tomorrow morning. The truck leaves this corner at four thirty in the morning and won't bring you back till suppertime. Bring water and pack some food. It's day-by-day work. Wages aren't as good as what the machinery guys are getting, but if you put in a day's work, you'll get a decent day's pay."

"Any cheap lodging nearby?" Hank asked.

"Try the Cordova on 8th and Figueroa. Rooms ain't too bad. Columbo's Italian Food and Steak House is right across the street. Tell the cook you're working on the stadium and he might pack lunches for you. He's a Dodgers fan. And tell him Johnnie sent you."

Hank walked several blocks to the Cordova. After five nights in the men's hostel, he was looking forward to some privacy. Meeting Johnnie was a stroke of luck. He'd take the cheapest room and the job in the San Fernando Valley for as long as it lasted and worry about applying for a green card later. Saving enough for tuition, housing, and living expenses would take a while, and it wasn't likely he'd be able to enroll for at least a year. Plenty of time to get his legal status looked after.

It seemed a lifetime ago since he'd left Saint John. Sometimes a wave of guilt and regret rose in his chest, nearly choking him with panic. He had stopped imagining Tanya's reaction when she woke to find him gone, a short note of apology on the bedside table. Jennifer probably stopped looking for him quite quickly.

Hank sat down on a bench, and the memory of Jennifer Dawn's first birthday came to mind. Her sweet full face was covered with frosting, and her little fists squeezed out handfuls of cake. She'd had another birthday since he left. Her blond hair was likely longer and maybe even curlier, but her dimpled smile and her giggling would probably sound the same as when she'd jumped in his arms every night when he walked through the door.

November 14, 2021

Hank turned the corner onto Duke. Mother used to take him to the little black house at the end of this street when he was young. Aunt Mae and Uncle Billy never had children of their own but received great-nieces and -nephews with genuine enthusiasm. Hank always felt such excitement going through their door to the pink peppermints, fizzy Sussex ginger ale, and a cake slathered in a frosting of brown sugar, butter, and coconut.

Stopping on the sidewalk looking at the front door, Hank's throat caught with emotion. The house looked the same, but the furnishings, photographs, trinkets, and the people inside would all be different, of course. Aunt Mae and Uncle Billy were long gone, and many others had inhabited this little black house, but the tug to open the door and enter was as strong as it had been when he was eight years old. Oh, for the feel of Aunt Mae's arms encircling him, her large bosom a cushion for a little boy's crewcut head. Oh, for Uncle Billy's strong back pats and exuberant "Who's this big boy? Can't be little Henry."

"We'll have to put a brick on his head to stop him from growing," Aunt Mae would chime in, her belly laugh shaking him before being released from the hug.

Hank loved that after all the hugging, teasing, and filling up on treats, he could sit in Uncle Billy's big chair and stare out at the water of Courtenay Bay. Sometimes the water would be high and sometimes the low tide would leave ripples of mud. He was mesmerized by it all, no matter the water level. To a boy from the north end, this was a different world. He would hear the chatter of the adults in the background but was content to spend the remainder of the visit just gazing out the big picture window.

Hank crossed the street and turned left. No warm house to enter or loving welcome waiting. These days his gaze at the waters of Courtenay

Bay was from the lower side of the causeway as he entered and exited the shelter he'd made a week ago: a large tarp slung over a shopping cart, held in place with a few spikes and weighted down with cement blocks. He couldn't stand up in his new home, but it kept him out of the wind and pretty much out of sight.

Waterfront property was not listed or shown by real estate agents like Miriam Ross, who had taken such pleasure in kicking him out of the rooming house. But at least he had a place to return to every night and a place to keep his belongings. Looking back at the little black house, Hank's eyes welled up. He would not walk past this house again. He'd find an alternate route at the end of each day.

1964

A bell rang as Hank pulled open the heavy door of the campus bookstore. Students with full baskets or armloads of books and supplies filled each aisle. The youthful exuberance made Hank feel ancient and out of place, although he probably was not much older than most of those milling about. He had just paid his first-term tuition and was officially enrolled in the sound engineering program at San Francisco State College. He pulled the book list from his dungaree pocket and reached for a basket.

Hank had arrived in San Francisco one week ago, and had been lucky to find a small room three blocks from campus. The room had a cot, a wardrobe, one chair, and a table big enough for a hotplate. He shared a bathroom with several others and had the use of a small kitchen with a refrigerator and a sink where he could wash his one plate, bowl, cup, fork, knife, and spoon.

"Oh, sorry," Hank said after bumping into two men at the end of the aisle, his apology a quick mumble.

"Not your fault, we're taking up the whole aisle," said the taller of the two men before planting a kiss squarely on his companion's lips.

"*Get a room*, he's probably thinking," the shorter man said.

"Sorry, I wasn't paying attention," Hank said, waving his book list in the air like a white flag. "I have no idea where to find anything."

"Give me your list, honey. Marcelle will help you. Follow me."

Hank fell in behind the two men. The taller man was beautiful, his blond hair pulled back in a ponytail accentuating his chiselled features and deep blue eyes. A loose-fitting, bright, colourful tunic covered his frame, flowing down to his sandalled feet. The other man had a more rugged, manly look. His light blue oxford shirt was a tight fit over his chest and the sleeves were rolled up, revealing muscular arms. Hank felt the colour rise in his neck and face and his heart rate quicken.

"I'm Raphael," the tall man turned back to say. "And this beautiful specimen is Roberto. Not the names our dear mothers gave us, but the names we've chosen to give ourselves. And life is all about choice, don't you think?"

Hank opened his mouth to respond, but not a sound came out. Swept up in the energy and sexuality of these two strangers, he realized how desperately lonely he was, how afraid and lost he felt even with everything he'd worked so hard for finally falling into place. He'd been holding his breath, moving through each day as if absent from his own body, keeping a tight lid on his feelings and desires for as long as he could remember. He felt a lump rise in his throat.

::

"Just throw your bags in the back of the van and we'll give you a drive to wherever you're headed," Raphael said as the three men walked out of the bookstore together a few minutes later. "Our kind must stick together. These streets aren't as friendly as you might think."

"It helps to have guys like you and Roberto among us," Raphael continued. "Some of the rest of us may as well carry a target on our backs. But I'm pretty good at recognizing our kind even when they don't look the part. I'm not wrong very often, and when I am it's more the guy's own denial than my misjudgment."

"Oh, I'm not a homosexual," Hank stammered.

"You keep telling yourself that, honey. Nobody's going to rush you."

November 15, 2021

H ank opened the inside door of the CIBC bank. The last time he'd tried
to use his debit card he had messed up and someone had to come
help him, so he'd just go to a teller today. The stares of the people in the
line ahead of him made him uncomfortable. His anger was mounting until
he realized it was probably because he wasn't wearing a mask. He mumbled an apology and a kind woman directly in front of him passed him a
face mask.

"It's brand new," the woman explained. "I carry several in my purse. It's
not the fancy N95 kind, but it will do. Who would have believed we'd all
be so nuts about covering our faces? My husband says we're all just sheep,
but I'm more of a rule follower. Always have been."

Hank took the mask, thanking the woman politely. He was used to
getting stares and dismissive looks from people. If only the looks were
just because his face wasn't covered.

"Do you have some identification, sir?"

Hank passed the teller his Medicare card and his vaccination passport.

"Nothing with your picture or present address?"

"I don't have a driver's licence," Hank replied. "I have my old Irving employee card, if that will do. It has my picture on it, although I'm much older
now."

"Is this your current address?"

Hank nodded.

"Sign this, please, sir."

Finally, after an uncomfortably long time, the teller counted out the
bills. Hank stuffed the money into his pocket, anxious to get out of there.
The whole ordeal had left him feeling nervous and vulnerable.

The cold air and sleet hit him as he stepped out onto the sidewalk. He
scanned the street up and down, looking for anyone who might have been

in the bank watching him. No one seemed to be paying him the least bit of attention or appeared threatening in any way. Later he'd separate the money into several different pockets and stuff a bill or two into his socks in case someone tried to rob him.

Hank walked around the corner onto Germain Street.

1964

Hank sat on the edge of his cot, finally allowing the feelings of the day to catch up with him. First of all, the reality of being enrolled in a program he'd dreamt about for so many years filled him with emotion almost every day. But today, instead of sitting in a classroom listening to a lecture or reading pages in a textbook, his instructor had taken Hank and one other student to Tower Records to actually witness firsthand the preliminary steps of creating a vinyl record.

They stood in the production room watching the craftsman pour a thin layer of molten wax onto a hot plate. He applied a flame, melting any bubbles or flaws, then passed a second flame over it, before allowing it to cool. Once the disc cooled, he lifted it off and passed it through a slot to the recording room.

The three men had then slipped into the back of the recording room and quietly taken their places out of the way. Hank had felt such euphoria entering that magical room. The ceiling light overhead shone down on the large metal turntable, giving it an ethereal presence in the room. A man approached, wax disc in hand, and placed it on the turntable with an air of reverence that had Hank holding his breath.

Hank then turned his attention to the balding man sitting at the sound board. Hank knew from his textbook the part that man and the knobs and mechanisms at his fingertips would play in what was to come next. The man over at the turntable adjusted the stylus, waiting for the sound engineer's mixing to achieve the best musical balance.

Next Hank heard the beginning strains of "The Blue Danube Waltz" and looked at the large ensemble of musicians sitting at the far end of the room. He'd been so mesmerized by the turntable and the impressive sound board, it was as if the musicians only appeared when the first note resonated. The vibrations of sound brought from the microphone passed through the cutting head to the stylus, the stylus cutting the vibrations into the soft wax, recording the tones forever.

Hank thought back to all the times he'd stood in Woolworths totally in awe of the albums he pulled from the racks. After selecting one or two, he'd carry them carefully on his bus ride home. He'd rush to his bedroom, then plug in and open the RCA Victor Victrola Phonograph he'd bought after saving his paper-route money for three years. Next, he'd tear off the cellophane from the first album and pull the vinyl record from the jacket. Just looking at the label and the concentric ridges brought an indescribable joy. Carefully he'd place the record on the turntable, lift the arm, and place the needle gently onto the first groove.

Hank had watched in awe today as the sound engineer played a pivotal role in producing the grooves on the soft wax and Hank saw firsthand how a vinyl record is made, making the recorded music available to hundreds of thousands of listeners. Just a cog in the massive wheel of the music industry, and he was now training to be a part of that magic.

November 15, 2021

"*M*y name is Pearl, and I'm an alcoholic. My name is Pearl, and I'm an alcoholic."

Pearl moved closer to the bathroom mirror. "My name is Pearl, and I'm an alcoholic."

Richard had called yesterday to tell her the meeting had been cancelled due to the...he'd said something about colour; red or orange, Pearl couldn't remember which, but no public meetings while New Brunswick was in it, whatever colour it was.

"You can go to online meetings, Pearl. Just Google 'AA Zoom meetings.'"

"I'll zoom right over to those, whatever the hell they are," Pearl muttered to herself, picking up the brush, hoping to tame her messed-up hair.

I don't have a fucking computer was what she'd wanted to say to Richard but had instead thanked him for calling and told him she'd figure something out. Did she even need a meeting? "You're only an arm's length away from your next drink," they always said. But she'd been sober for more than seven years and had never once felt the desire to even buy a bottle, let alone open it, pour a drink, and put it to her lips. Remembering the taste of rye whiskey, her old drink of choice, made her stomach churn.

Was it the meetings she was craving? Was it the steps, slogans, and pats on the back she needed? She loved that people there knew her by name. Before this damn pandemic the people at meetings touched her, hugged her, patted her on the back, spoke to her, and listened to her. People saw her and cared if she was there or not. If she missed a meeting someone always called. Phyllis brought her casseroles or baking every week. Donald showed her pictures of his grandchildren. Theodore had given her one of his wife's paintings last Christmas. Mike called her his hero, his inspiration.

"I'm Pearl, and I'm an alcoholic."

Pearl slammed the brush down and walked out to the kitchen. Looking out at the ice-covered sidewalk, she realized she hadn't been outside for three days. She'd fallen on a dry sidewalk a few weeks ago, so she damn sure wasn't going to venture out on an icy one. Thankfully, she'd made a trip to Giant Tiger her last day out and had stocked up. She still had enough food in the house.

Did anyone even realize they hadn't seen the old lady walk by their windows? Did the guy in the apartment on the ground floor even notice she'd not been down her stairs or opened the creaking door? She could be dead, for goodness' sake, and not a soul would know.

Pearl pulled a saucepan from the cupboard. Tomato soup and crackers. The dinner of champions. She remembered how pleased she'd been as a kid when there was milk enough to add to the can instead of water. She opened the fridge and, shaking the carton, realized it would be water added to this can. No milk in the soup if she wanted to have enough for her coffee tomorrow morning. If the day warmed up enough to melt the ice, she'd venture down the street to the corner store. She liked the owner. He was always friendly. Maybe she'd even introduce herself.

"I'm Pearl, and I'm an alcoholic." Pearl chuckled.

1964

Annette Lowman decided when the phone started ringing that she just wouldn't answer it. She'd had a migraine since early morning and talking on the phone was the last thing she needed. Mavis often called at this time of day, and getting off the phone in under an hour with her was a feat, but on the seventh ring, Annette picked up the phone.

"Mom?"

"Henry? Is that you?"

The line was silent, and for a second Annette wondered if she'd imagined her son's voice.

"Yeah, Mom, it's me. I've been trying to call George, but he's not answering. I wondered if you had his grandmother's phone number."

"I'm the telephone directory now, am I? I haven't heard from you in four years and the only thing you have to say is you want Ida Murphy's telephone number. You're lucky your father wasn't home to answer."

"Sorry, Mom. I'm just a bit worried about George. I have a bad feeling."

"How about the feeling I've had since the day you disappeared? Your father and I were humiliated that our son would leave his wife and little girl without a thought for his responsibilities. I'm sure the Bennetts think we're just north end trash, raising a son who would do such a thing. We've tried to keep in touch with Jennifer, but we've been pushed out of her life because of what you did. Your father will never get over it, Henry. And poor Grannie, she died of a broken heart after such a shameful thing."

"I'm sorry, Mom. I know you can't understand why I did what I did. I just need George's grandmother's phone number. She still lives next door, doesn't she? I need to find out if George is all right."

Annette shifted the receiver to her other ear and pressed two fingers to her throbbing temple. "Well, I can tell you he isn't. It happened a month or so ago. Washed overboard, they say. I never understood why you were so keen on him anyway. He was never right. Mavis says he was light in the loafers. They never found his body, so maybe he wasn't on the boat at all. Maybe he faked his death so he could go live somewhere with other men like him. I don't think Ida Murphy needs a call from you. I'm sure it's hard enough without you stirring everything up."

Waiting for a response, she realized the way she told Henry about George hadn't been very kind. "I'm sorry, Henry. I'm sure it's a shock, but you did ask me." Annette paused again. "Are you there, Henry? Well goodness' sake, you finally call and then hang up without so much as a goodbye. Did you run out of change for the pay phone or what?" She coughed. "Henry? Don't even bother calling back," Annette said, raising her voice to a shout, as if that would ensure her son got the message before she slammed the receiver down.

November 15, 2021

Gloria pulled the paint palate closer, envisioning the pail the little boy was holding to be yellow. As her brush hovered over the tray, she remembered what colour it had been. She dipped her brush in the red paint, but before guiding it to the canvas she stopped, set the brush in the water, pulled her stool out, and reached for a tissue to wipe the tears from her cheeks.

She stepped back and looked at the painting. A little boy on the beach. Not alone or unattended. She had painted a woman's arm, shoulder, and sandalled foot on the edge of the painting to show that the little boy was not alone, that the mother was there. *Showing who?* Gloria asked herself out loud, the emotion in the words ramping her tears to a steady flow.

It had been just her and Zachary that day. He'd filled his little red pail over and over, creating the elaborate waterways in the sand at the edge of the rippling water. His pudgy toes and short, tanned legs toddled across the beach while she lay outstretched on a blanket nearby. He had been fine, happy and laughing, crying only when she told him it was time to leave. She recalled picking him up mid-tantrum and carrying him to the path leading up to the house. Looking back, she saw they'd left the bucket behind and she scurried back to get it, hoping the crying would not start up again.

During the years that followed, she spent so many more days on that beautiful shore by the river, and as each child came along, the red bucket passed from hand to hand. She'd been a good mother, never leaving them unattended or in any danger. She'd applied the sunscreen and made them wear their life jackets until they became strong and able swimmers. She'd packed the snacks and drinks.

Gloria's sobs intensified as she moved across the room to the finished paintings hanging on the pegboard wall. In one beach painting, four chil-

SUCH A WINTER'S DAY

dren surrounded a mother dancing in the rippling water. In another, the black water was illuminated with the last rays of a setting sun, and three grown children were sitting on the beach. No mother in the painting. And no amount of care or worry had prevented the accident that took the life of the absent sibling.

Why was the memory of that day at the beach so raw and painful? Her first-born child, her precious little boy, had not toddled back to the water. Zachary had not been carried away by waves. That day and that danger were not what had taken her oldest son. Her son at twenty had died on the roadside in an accident caused by poor choices and circumstance. But sometimes she was flooded with the gripping guilt of that, as if she'd let a small boy enter deep water unattended.

The shrill doorbell Ted had installed brought Gloria back to the present moment. "You don't want just anyone walking in, Gloria," he'd said as he wired it in. "You'd be so busy painting you wouldn't even hear someone sneaking in. They could rob you blind and leave you for dead. Keep the door locked. This doorbell will alert you and you can decide who to let in." She wiped her eyes and cheeks, and headed into the hall to see who was at the door.

An attractive, well-dressed woman began speaking as she pushed her way through the open door, wrestling her umbrella closed. "I thought maybe you weren't here, even though your sign says you're open. I had to practically step over a man sprawled out on your step. I told him in no uncertain terms that this city has vagrancy laws. Did you know he was there? I doubt he's an art connoisseur. You won't get much business with the likes of him blocking your door. I expect it's the overhang that's the attraction. It's just terrible trying to walk down this block. There's several with their hands out in front of the bank, and there's always that scary looking guy sitting in front of the old Bustin's playing the guitar. I just keep on walking. I don't work as hard as I do to support every pathetic soul I see. If I did, I wouldn't have a cent left."

"It's a wet one today," Gloria said. "Almost snow. And a cold wind. My heart breaks for those folks with no warm place out of the weather."

"There's plenty of warm places. They choose not to go. Don't want to have to follow the rules, I figure."

Turning away from the woman to close the door, Gloria took a deep breath, resisting the urge to engage in a discussion. "Would you like to take your wet coat off?" she asked. "I can hang it here in the hall if you'd like."

"That would be lovely. Would you have a place I could fix my hair? For all the good it will do. I only have a minute. I'm looking for a particular piece I saw on your Facebook page. A beach painting. I just sold a client a lovely big home in the valley, right by the Renforth wharf, and I want to take her a small gift as a thank you."

Gloria read the business card the woman passed her. *Miriam Ross, RE/MAX.*

1964

*P*earl closed the door, hoping to dull the cries coming from the crib. There was not a thing wrong with that child, except for maybe the fact he had such a loser for a mother. The first few months had been almost manageable, and she'd tried her best to do everything right. She had even nursed the baby, although everyone was saying bottle feeding was the modern way. And it wasn't like she got any credit for doing it. Certainly not from Vince, who seemed to get angrier and angrier about it as the months passed.

"Is that kid going to be hanging off your tit till he goes to school?"

Weaning hadn't been easy, but David was drinking from a cup now, and eating everything she gave him. But breastfeeding had kept her from drinking. She'd stopped right away when she found out she was pregnant and had stayed away from the whiskey the whole time she nursed the baby. She'd gotten no credit for that either, except Vince being happy it left more for him.

Pearl took the bottle opener from the drawer and popped the top off the bottle of ginger ale. It always reminded her of visits to Grannie's house on Needham Street. Grannie would fill a large tumbler with Sussex ginger ale, and except for occasional trips to the Riv with her dad, Pearl wasn't used to having soda pop. She always loved putting the glass up to her mouth, knowing that before she even took a sip the bubbles would make her sputter and cough.

When had that sputter and cough started coming from the strong taste of alcohol? Pearl dropped ice cubes into the tumbler and poured in whiskey before adding the ginger ale.

The crying seemed to be getting louder. Surely he'd fall asleep if she waited long enough. Taking a big swig, Pearl left the kitchen and walked down the hall. If she sat out on the fire escape, she wouldn't hear the crying, and wouldn't have to look around at this dump she was stuck in day after day. Seventeen years old, saddled with a kid and hitched to exactly the kind of man she'd always promised herself she'd never marry. Who could blame her for having a good stiff drink? Maybe after one or two she could stomach filling up the wringer washer and finally getting to the pile of dirty diapers.

"This goddamned place stinks like the sewer," Vince hollered before he'd slammed the door. "Teach that kid to shit in the toilet, would you?"

November 16, 2021

J enny Lowman circled the parking lot, looking for a space close to the steps. Most days she didn't mind parking a distance away, but with today's rain she would get soaked on the long walk into the hospital. Her mother had been admitted three weeks ago. Yesterday the doctor had discussed palliative care with them, and for the first time it hit her that her mother was losing her battle with the cancer she'd been diagnosed with two years ago. But just like this rain, there was not a damn thing she could do about it.

Jenny pressed the up arrow on the wall beside the elevators. Up, when really she wanted to be anywhere but here. She wanted to sprint out through the lobby and back out the revolving doors to the sidewalk. She hated hospitals. She hated the smell, the suffocating dead air, and the stream of silent, sad, desperate people either ill themselves or visiting their sick loved ones. Everyone seemed to be going through the motions, following arrows and memorized paths toward suffering and agony. Zombie-like masked people weighed down with stuffed animals, balloons, bouquets, and Tim Hortons cups and bags as they filed through the corridors and in and out of the elevators.

A well-dressed woman nearly knocked into Jenny, shifting her large purse and several bags as the elevator door opened.

"Take the steps, my therapist says. Good for the mind and the body. Bullshit, I say. The stairwell smells like they drop dead bodies down from each floor to the morgue below."

The chatty woman pushed the button. Jenny moved toward the back of the elevator as more people got on. The woman continued talking, her comments not directed at anyone.

"I hate this damn place. But if you're the only one still living around here when your mom's on her way out, they all guilt you into visiting her.

Like she even cares. She's got it better in here than she had all her sad, sorry life. She bosses the nurses around as if they're her own personal staff. She's watched too much *Downton Abbey*. She's got it in her addled mind that she's the lady of the manor."

No one in the elevator responded to the woman's continual chatter except for a nod here and there. The door opened and Jenny followed the woman out.

"Sorry. I do go on. It's my nerves, my therapist tells me. I think it's my line of work. I sell real estate, and you have to be a talker and a real bull-shitter to sell houses, even with the market as good as it is right now. Are you visiting someone?"

"Yeah, my mom," Jenny answered. "She's not doing well."

"Oh, I am so sorry. My mom's not doing well either. I love my mom, don't get me wrong, but I could count on one hand the number of times she went out her way for me. I broke my arm once, and she made me wait until the next day to go to the hospital when my aunt could drive me. She couldn't possibly pay for a taxi to take me to St. Joe's. But here I am, the good daughter who comes every day to see her. 'Let Mary do it,' they all say. 'Mary will do it.'"

The woman stopped, turned, and extended her hand. "Miriam Ross, by the way."

1964

Hank lifted his head from the arm of the couch. The floor was pretty much covered with sprawling bodies in various stages of undress. He couldn't remember falling asleep, but he did recall the euphoria he'd felt after being passed the bong. The whole evening had been surreal. In a good way, mostly, even though Raphael had brought him to the party kicking and screaming.

"Listen here, honey. You must get out more. Live a little. Who knows, you might find the man of your dreams."

In the two months since meeting Raphael, Hank had made no headway in convincing him he had no interest in men.

"There'll be lots of lovely ladies there too, Hank. Some might even fool you. Some gorgeous ladies have the goods under all that glamour. It'll be like Christmas. Do some unwrapping and see what you get."

In trying to sit himself up Hank realized he wasn't alone on the couch. The vibrant pink gown had ridden up and two fishnet-covered legs were draped over his. The red wig had come off and the early morning light revealed the stubble that layers of foundation and rouge had covered last night.

"Good morning, Canada."

Hank pulled himself up to a sitting position and focused, unsure of his physical state. His head felt groggy, his mouth was dry, and his stomach was roiling.

"Let's get out of here and go have some breakfast. If you think I'm overdressed, I have other clothes. Funny how what seems perfect once the sun goes down or the stage lights go up scares the shit out of folks in the light of day.

"How'd you know I'm Canadian?"

"East coast is my guess. We think it's everyone else with accents, but the truth is, ours is just as distinctive."

"Ours? Where are you from?"

"I hail from the Bible belt of New Brunswick. Not a great fit for me, as you might guess. You New Brunswick too? Don't hear Newfoundland or Cape Breton."

"Yeah, Saint John."

"Well, ain't that something? Two NB boys winding up on the same settee in sunny California. Breakfast?"

November 17, 2021

*L*iam grabbed his bagged lunch from the staff room refrigerator. It was going to be a busy afternoon and a long night. He loved the challenge of a concert like this, but the baby had been awake several times in the night and it had been his turn to go to her. He only had about twenty minutes to eat—though he really needed some fresh air and sunshine. Sitting on a bench in King's Square to eat lunch seemed like a perfect idea.

Any time spent people watching in King's Square was good as far as Liam was concerned. Before sitting down, Liam scanned the square looking for Hank. In the last two weeks he'd seen him several times and always enjoyed their conversations about bands and musicians. Today he'd brought the album cover they'd talked about last time, and he really hoped Hank would be sitting on his regular bench.

Liam had been sitting a few minutes when he spotted Hank crossing the street. Wrapping the remainder of his sandwich, Liam stood and started along the sidewalk to meet him. Hank's step quickened and a smile broadened on his face when he saw Liam approach.

"How you doing, Hank? Amanda packed me a big lunch today, and I'd be more than happy to share what's left."

Together the two men walked to their regular bench in full view of the Imperial. Liam pulled out the wrapped sandwich and passed it to Hank.

"What a great lad you are. Does Amanda know you feed more than the pigeons most days?"

"I've told her all about my lunch buddy," Liam said, passing Hank the sandwich. "She can't wait to meet you."

Hank unwrapped the cellophane and took a bite. "Right, I'm sure she's waiting with bated breath to meet some old bum you met sitting on a bench in King's Square."

"She is, actually. The album cover I told you about is hers. She is a big Harry Chapin fan. One of my brother's best friends was named after him, actually. Most people know 'Taxi' or 'Cat's in the Cradle,' but I think his lesser-known story songs are the best."

Liam took the album out of the bag and passed it to Hank.

"*Anthology of Harry Chapin*. Well, isn't that something now. Album covers are a work of art. I was always in awe of the work that went into creating one. Not that I had anything to do with that part of it, but I was always anxious to see what package the artist chose to carry their vinyl."

Hank flipped the album over, squinted his eyes, and moved it closer.

"Print's too small for these old eyes," Hank said, passing the album back to Liam.

Liam considered reading the two columns to Hank but instead typed "Remember When the Music" into his phone and pushed play. Both men sat in silence, letting the song play out fully. Liam felt the gentle shake of the bench. Tears streamed down Hank's cheeks. Liam passed Hank a napkin, waiting silently, feeling a sacredness in what they'd just shared.

"Now that fella knew what music was," Hank said. "Not everyone does, you know. I figure you do, being in the business you're in. You make music happen for folks. Bought my first record right over there. Used to be Woolworths. Had to save up for weeks to buy the damn thing, but it was worth every penny."

Liam pulled a muffin from the lunch bag, split it, and passed Hank half, waiting for him to continue his story.

"He died in a car accident on the Long Island Expressway, didn't he?" Hank asked.

"1981, I think, although the eighties are a little foggy for me. Buddy Holly, plane crash, 1959, I remember all those details. And then there's the famous 27 Club, 1970, Janis Joplin and Jimi Hendrix both dead at age twenty-seven. So many singers gone too soon. Mama Cass one of them, for sure."

"Didn't Mama Cass choke on a ham sandwich or something?"

"Not true. The poor woman had a heart attack."

"My mother always told us not to eat lying down, warning us we'd choke like Mama Cass," Liam said.

"That's the way legends start and myths take on a life of their own. No, Cass Elliot had a heart attack. Her lifestyle wasn't healthy; show after show, no sleep, and all the other crap that went with it."

"Oh shit, I've got to get back to work," Liam said. "Same time tomorrow, Hank?"

"Sure, why not?"

Hank took the last bite of muffin as he watched Liam run across the street to the theatre. "I knew her, you know," Hank said out loud, to no one.

1966

Hank pulled his jeans on and grabbed the wrinkled shirt he'd discarded carelessly when they'd stumbled into bed last night. His decision to meet Marvin at the club was stupid enough, but the choice to keep drinking and be the last ones pushed out the door was what he was paying for this morning. He'd waited six months for today's opportunity, so why had that not kept him from being so damn stupid?

Hank had dreamt of a job like the one he was starting today at United Western Recorders. Todd had been impressed with his marks and his references, but Hank knew he'd been hired as a gopher. The Mamas & the Papas had a recording session this morning, and just being present for that was amazing. Maybe before long he'd be sitting at the board. But being late his first day wouldn't help.

Hank pulled the outside door tight, checking to make sure it was locked, and ran down the street. The planter beside the bus stop was overflowing with a mix of flowers and garbage, beauty and refuse. Everything California seemed to be. Daisies always reminded him of the day Tanya walked down the aisle toward him. He'd recited the meaningless vows with a knot of regret and terror in his gut and a fake smile on his face. And six months later, when they put his daughter in his arms, he still hadn't faced the truth.

November 18, 2021

Bruce Smith drove the City Works truck slowly, looking for a parking spot close to Backstreet Records. An addiction, Edna had called it, as she watched his record collection expanding in the first few years of their marriage. But Bruce remembered how happy Edna had been when he brought home the fancy TV and stereo console from Bustin's the first year they were married. She loved placing her Beatles and Elvis records on the turntable or tuning in to *Front Page Challenge* on the black-and-white television.

But she criticized his careless spending when the records in the stand beside the console moved to shelves in the basement rec room, taking over one complete wall. He'd parted with most of his albums when he moved into the small apartment, the last holdout his Bob Dylan collection. But today he was seeing what Gordie Tufts might give him for five of them. It was probably ridiculous to hang on to them when he could listen to most anything on YouTube.

It wasn't the same, but not many people got that. Who even cared what the process had been to make vinyl records? More and more he felt out of touch, a dinosaur, a relic of the past, and that feeling only intensified when he'd tried explaining the amazing process of making vinyl records to one of his coworkers the other day. He may as well have been speaking Chinese. Troy hadn't been the least bit interested in hearing how the master matrix, the mother matrix, and the stampers were made. Even the fact that the disc was initially placed in a chamber with a block of pure gold hadn't impressed Troy enough to keep listening.

Bruce parked the truck and picked up the albums off the seat. *Before the Flood* from 1974, *Hard Rain* from 1976, *Street Legal* from 1978, *Shot of Love* from 1981, and *Oh Mercy* from 1989. The oldest albums would be worth the most, but there were some he refused to part with. He wasn't hard up enough to let *Dylan and the Dead* go.

Bruce was not entirely convinced he was going into Back Street today. He'd sit here a while longer. Glancing in the rear-view mirror, Bruce noticed the man approaching on the sidewalk. It was the man he'd spoken to in the Loyalist Burial Ground a week or so ago. He turned the key in the ignition so he could lower the driver's window.

"Hey. Where you going?" Bruce hollered.

The man stopped abruptly, quickly registering where the voice was coming from and that the question had been directed at him.

"Hank, right?" Bruce continued. "We met the other day. It's a raw one, isn't it? I'm just killing a bit of time. Want to hop in out of the cold for a bit?"

"Yeah, sure."

Bruce moved the stuff off the passenger seat, still clutching the five albums. Had his reluctance to sell these treasured items prompted his invitation? It was cold out there, and there was no harm in letting the guy get warm for a few minutes. Bruce started up the engine and turned the heat up.

"I'm on my lunch break, just running an errand," Bruce said. "Avoiding an errand, really. Thought I might try to sell these to the guy at Backstreet Records."

"Dylan, eh? Sure you want to part with them?"

Bruce passed the stack of albums to Hank.

"Well, that's just the thing. I don't," Bruce answered. "Thought I might get a few bucks for them, though."

"I worked on some of his early stuff," Hank said.

"You what?" Bruce asked, not sure he'd heard the old guy right.

"Dylan recorded mostly in New York, but I worked on some of his California recordings. 'Knockin' on Heaven's Door' was recorded in Santa Monica. I hadn't paid my dues yet, so I wasn't credited on that recording, but I worked the board some, for the album it was on. I was part of history."

"Oh my god, you're kidding."

Bruce looked over at the man sitting across from him. Hank had slipped off his hood as the truck got warmer, showing a head of white hair nearly long enough to tie back in a ponytail. His beard was nearly as white, his face wrinkled, but those deep blue eyes were twinkling. How many people even noticed those eyes or took the time to talk to this man?

"I wouldn't let these go if I was you," Hank said. "Wish I still had all my vinyl. Nothing like it. God, kids think they know what music is these days, but how many of them have a clue how astounding and intricate the process of producing a vinyl record was back in the day?"

"Holy shit, Hank," Bruce said. "I was just trying to tell someone about that process yesterday. He didn't have a clue what I was talking about. Not many folks do, I guess. Some of the guys remember CDs, but the younger ones only know all that digital shit and most haven't got a clue about the science of creating music on vinyl, even though it seems to be making a comeback."

"Oh yeah CDs, cassettes, and the eight track before that. The beginning of the end as far as I'm concerned."

Hank passed the stack of albums back to Bruce, embarrassed that he'd gotten so wound up. Looking out to sidewalk he noticed the same three high school kids who'd peppered him earlier with a string of insults walk by. The warmth which seconds ago felt so welcome suddenly felt stifling and oppressive, and Hank considered jumping out of the truck.

"It's like I was meant to run into you today," Bruce said. "There's no way I'm selling these. So what if I can't take them with me? I'm not dead yet. I just might start popping in to Back Street to build up my collection again."

"Sounds like a great plan to me. If you still have something decent to play these on when you get home tonight, put the *Hard Rain* album on. 'Shelter from the Storm' is the track right after 'Lay Lady Lay.' Shut your eyes and listen to Dylan's words, his voice. Listen to the drums and percussion, the repetitive guitar riffs accentuating the lyrics and mournful lament for comfort and acceptance. That track gets overlooked in the shadow of 'Lay Lady Lay,' but it's a classic.

Bruce couldn't believe what he was hearing. "You are an unsung treasure walking the sidewalks of this city. How was I lucky enough to run into you?"

1967

H ank looked at his paycheque before folding it and putting it into the pocket of his jeans. Hard to believe he'd been at United a year already. Even harder to believe he and Marvin had been together that long. At first, he'd been sure Marvin was a passing fling—a dalliance, Raphael called it, discouraging Hank from settling down.

"You've got to play the field, darling," Raphael had said the day Hank had finally admitted his sexual preferences and his attraction to Marvin, shortly after Raphael had introduced them. "And all those want-to-be Mia Farrows you've been dating don't count. You've been dipping your toes into streams leading down to an ocean you have no desire to be swimming in. Jump in the deep end, and you'll find your sea legs."

Hank smiled at the memory but at the same time swallowed the lump in his throat that always surfaced every time memories of Raphael came to mind. What a shock it had been when Roberto came to tell them that Raphael was gone. Back to Wisconsin, for goodness' sake, and back to being Ralph Johnston. A choice he made apparently with the incentive of inheriting his family's fortune.

But what had that choice meant to the ones he left behind, the ones who'd found their own strength and courage from the bravery and self-confidence Raphael emitted? But maybe it was Raphael leaving San Francisco that had pushed Hank to commit more seriously to his relationship with Marvin. Hank had been passing all his life and hiding behind that safety. Marvin was just the opposite, flamboyantly wearing who he was in his demeanour, his gait, and his clothing. After Raphael left, Hank had made the choice to no longer deny who he was and who he loved.

But even after making that choice, and he and Marvin being together for a year, Hank still felt the wisest approach was to keep their affection for one another behind closed doors. Marvin, however, strongly disagreed.

"I'm taking my man out on the town to celebrate tonight," Marvin declared, walking into the room and twirling Hank around for a kiss. "And, my love, you will watch me walking down the aisle toward you someday when we make this union official. You've got me for life, Canada."

"You're living in a dream world, Marv."

"I would rather dream than give in to the narrow-minded, intolerant bastards who think we should be given lobotomies, castrated, put in mental institutions, or pistol whipped. Change will never come unless we are brave enough to own who we are, love who we love, and wear what we damn well want to wear."

Hank stepped back, surveying Marvin's outfit. "Does that always have to include a pink boa, red lipstick, and heels?" Hank asked. "Wear comfortable shoes if nothing else. Pretty damn hard to run from the thugs in four-inch spiked heels."

"You wear what you want to wear, Canada. God knows I find your James Dean look very appealing."

November 19, 2021

*G*loria slipped on her coat and boots. She'd only just realized how hungry she was, having been totally absorbed in the painting she was working on. The front of the City Market held such beauty and detail. Her interpretation was recognizable, but the abstract quality was what she was going for. She would take a break, walk over, and purposefully enter the market from Charlotte Street, paying attention to the entrance. She'd grab some lunch on her outing, bring it back, and continue working.

Walking through the square a little while later, Gloria recognized the man sitting on a bench facing the Imperial Theatre. She'd seen him sitting on her stoop a few times and yesterday had noticed him standing looking at her window display.

Gloria thought back to the rant Miriam Ross had delivered two days ago when she'd complained about stepping over him to get in the door. Gloria still felt a pang of guilt for her silence. She approached the bench and sat beside the man. She shifted her purse and reached into the brown paper bag to pull out her sandwich.

"Hello," Gloria said. "Nice day, isn't it?"

"Great day," the man replied.

"I hadn't planned on eating my lunch here, but it's such a beautiful day. We don't get many of these this late in the fall. I was going to take my lunch back to my art studio on Germain. I'm working on a painting of the City Market, so I thought, why not just pop up and grab a sandwich from Jeremiah's. Would you like half? It's ham and cheese." Gloria felt slightly embarrassed by her incessant chatter but kept talking. "Jeremiah's does make a good sandwich. I've had their tuna salad and it's good. Really, I've never had anything there I didn't like. You're more than welcome to half."

"No thanks. That's very nice of you, but a young fella gave me some of his lunch just a bit ago, so I'm good. I don't sit here waiting for folks to feed me, just so you know. The young fella is a new friend of mine. He works over there," the man said, pointing toward the Imperial Theatre.

Gloria nodded, taking a bite of the sandwich. She opened the small flap of the takeout coffee cup and took a sip while the man kept talking.

"He eats his lunch here most days, and, God love him, he's been sharing some of it with me."

"My sister-in-law volunteers there," Gloria said. "She takes the tickets and shows folks to their seats. And in return she gets to see the show for free."

"Sounds like a good deal for her," Hank said.

Gloria had another bite of the sandwich, the silence feeling a bit awkward.

"You have an art studio, you say?"

"Yes. On what they used to call the Quality Block on Germain. My name is Gloria, by the way."

"I'm Hank. I've seen your paintings in the window. They're real nice. You're a talented lady."

Gloria pulled the second half of the sandwich from the wrapper. "Well, thank you. I don't know how talented I am, but I do love painting the local landmarks. This is a beautiful city."

"It has its nice parts for sure, like most places, I guess. I grew up here and couldn't leave soon enough. After coming back, I started to appreciate its beauty. Always the way, isn't it? You don't appreciate what you've got till you don't have it anymore."

"What part of the city did you grow up in?"

"The north end, Adelaide Street. But my Gran lived on the west side."

"I grew up on the west side. City Line. Funny, isn't it, how territorial we all are about the areas we grew up in. East side, south end, west side, north end. Strong loyalties and rivalry in it all. I live out of the city now over on the Kingston Peninsula, but I lived for a year in the south end a while ago, which to some of my west side friends was practically treason. Not to mention my country friends and my own kids, who figured I'd lost my mind completely. Whereabouts are you living?"

Hank didn't answer. "Your painting looking over to the west side from Tin Can Beach caught my eye. Spent a lot of time down there as a kid. Used to think my gran could look right over across the water and see me smoking or whatever shenanigans I was up to."

Gloria took another sip of her coffee. She was in no hurry to get back to her studio. "I was quite happy with how that painting turned out," she said. "I do tend to gravitate toward beach pictures, although I'm enjoying painting buildings these days. Next time come in and have a closer look. I have the Tin Can Beach painting on postcards; I'd love to give you one."

"Well, that would be really kind of you. Lovely talking to you, Gloria," Hank said, rising to his feet.

"And nice talking to you, Hank."

Hank shuffled away slowly. Gloria took the last sip of coffee. She crumpled up the sandwich wrapper and stuffed it into the paper bag along with the empty cup. She stood up and walked toward a nearby garbage can. A group of kids almost knocked into her.

"Look at that fucking loser," one boy said, pointing at Hank.

"This city sucks," another one said.

"His name is Hank," Gloria muttered under her breath as she walked in the opposite direction. "And you suck."

1968

H ank picked up the needle, playing the part with the repeated words over again, explaining the mistake to Marvin.

"A happy accident, Bones called it, and didn't put the blame where it should have been. I punched in too early. It's right at the 2:45 mark."

"What difference?" Marvin said. "Nobody but you guys would even notice. You get yourself all worked up over nothing."

"Right, like you never freak out when a false eyelash falls off or your lipstick smudges."

"Well, that's real art, sweetie. My face is nothing to play around with. The teeny boppers will buy up that single and the album will fly off the shelves. Nobody will be horrified that Denny Doherty seems to have a stutter."

"Right. Your vocation is groundbreaking. I just put sounds together, fit in percussion and bass, and make the vocals pop. My work doesn't matter."

"Oh, stop your whining and get over here."

"Lou said to leave it in."

"Well, if the great Lou Adler said it was okay, I don't know what you're fretting about."

"I'm not fretting. Is it so bad, wanting to share work stuff with you? You drag me to every show of yours and I act interested."

"Drag you? Love the play on words, Canada. Sorry I'm such a diva. I'm proud of you, you know. I tell everyone my man knows the Mamas & the Papas. Terrance is doing a Mama Cass number in his set. He can pull off a psychedelic tent dress and beehive with the best of them."

November 20, 2021

Pearl passed the envelope to the girl behind the counter. Earlier, when she'd taken the money from the slot at the bank machine, she'd quickly stuffed it in the envelope and dropped it in her old purse. She hardly ever used the bank machine and wasn't sure the numbers she'd punched in were even her code, but they'd worked. After withdrawing the cash, she caught the bus to McAllister Place.

Yesterday she'd decided she would buy an iPad. She'd even called Aliant this morning asking about getting internet. She was stepping right into the twenty-first century, she'd told herself after hanging up. All this just so she could start going to those online AA meetings Richard kept telling her about.

"You need the support, Pearl," he'd said. "I know you think you've got sobriety all wrapped up, but we need each other. And just think how much you have to offer others who are just starting their journey."

"Would you like tech support? How about an extended warranty?" the girl asked.

"How about someone just show me how to turn the damn thing on?" Pearl replied.

"Oh, it's all straightforward. Most folks your age get their grandchildren to show them." The cashier passed Pearl back some twenties and the envelope.

Pearl stuffed the bills into her wallet and put the Source bag into the large blue purse. What a stupid, cumbersome thing a purse was. She never carried one and like her mother, kept her money in her bra, even when she walked down to Giant Tiger for groceries. The crazy old lady would be a perfect target for purse snatchers, but no one wanted to venture anywhere near her undergarments.

Pearl walked toward the food court. She would treat herself to lunch before catching the bus back uptown. Big day all around.

::

Pearl spotted Hank seated across the square as the bus rounded the corner. She had run into him a few times since the day he'd helped her off the sidewalk. Some days when she ran into him, he was the only living person she spoke to, and she always came away from their chats feeling better.

Pearl shuffled to the front of the bus as it stopped. She exited, walked to the corner, and waited for the pedestrian light.

"Pearl, hello," Hank called out and she crossed.

"Good day to you, Hank."

"Are you going to sit for a bit? Where you coming from?" Hank asked.

"I was at the mall. Bought myself an iPad today."

"Well, aren't you the one?"

"Oh, I'm the one all right. I'm even getting the Wi-Fi. I'm getting it for Zoom meetings. AA Zoom meetings."

"I know what AA is, but what the hell are Zoom meetings?"

"I'm no expert, but apparently, I can go to an AA meeting anywhere in the world. I'd much rather just go to the one I'm used to, but with this damn pandemic, we haven't been having them."

"I'd like to say I'm not interested in such things as the internet, but that wouldn't be quite true. My friend Liam has shown me some amazing things his phone will do, so I can only imagine what I could do with a computer or one of those pads. He played me a Grateful Dead concert yesterday."

"Well, maybe you should invest in one, a phone or an iPad. If I can, I'm sure you can."

"I'd go and buy it, and the next thing some punk would be stealing it from me. And pretty sure I'd need electricity to charge the damn thing. Don't have that luxury where I'm hanging my hat these days."

"That's a darn shame, Hank. It's not right."

"Lots about this old world ain't right."

"That's the God's truth. Brighter days ahead, right?"

"That's my motto."

1969

$\mathcal{P}$earl frantically moved through the flat, pushing clothes under the ratty couch, shoving garbage into Dominion store bags and scooping up the dirty dishes. She'd rushed home in a panic for fear they'd get there before her and would realize she'd left Kenny and Ruthie home alone. They were both still sound asleep when she'd left to walk David to school, and a good mother wouldn't let a six-year-old walk these streets by himself. Mr. Reicker had met her at the door, ushering David in before dropping the news.

"Child Protection has been called, Mrs. Higgins. David's teacher has come to me on several occasions saying that you have been drunk when picking him up after school. She is also concerned that David comes most days without a proper lunch and often is not dressed suitably for the weather. You have two little ones at home, do you not? Who stays with them when you're not home?"

Pearl had mumbled a reply and left immediately. Coming in the door, she'd put Ruthie in the high chair and tied Kenny to a kitchen chair. No milk meant their cereal would be dry, but picking up Cheerios a fistful at a time would keep them busy while she tried to get the flat looking more presentable.

November 22, 2021

Hearing the doorbell ring, Gloria looked through the small window in the door. She recognized the man she'd spoken to in the square a few days ago. She opened the door, feeling the gust of cold air.

"Hank, isn't it?" Gloria asked.

"Yes. You have a good memory."

"Not so sure about that," Gloria replied. "Come in out of the cold. I'll put the kettle on if you've got time for tea."

"Always time for tea, or a cuppa as my gran would say."

"Was she British?"

"Yeah. A war bride from the First World War."

"She's the one you said lived over west."

"That's right. You do have a good memory, to recall what some old guy was rambling on about."

"I'm glad you stopped in. I'll look for that postcard after I make the tea."

Gloria gestured for Hank to hang his coat on the hooks before leaving the hallway.

"You're not afraid I'll rob you blind while you're putting the kettle on?" Hank called out as he unzipped his coat.

"Now, why would I worry about that?" Gloria said, returning to the doorway of the kitchen.

"Folks see me and think the worst," Hank answered. "I'm just a scary homeless guy, so of course I'm a thief and can't be trusted."

"Well, I trust you. Milk or sugar?"

"Just tea would be great."

1969

J enny stared out the window as her grandfather drove onto the highway. Last night's call had changed her plans, which had been to spend
the day with Valerie and Debbie at the pool. Instead, she had been forced
to go on this outing with her grandparents. Of course, Ricky and Roger
didn't have to go, because Grammie and Grampie Lowman weren't their
grandparents.

"They'll likely take you to the Timberland, and you love their banana
splits, Jenny." Jenny knew there was no point arguing with her mother.

"Mavis and Tom took their grandchildren to Animal Land last week,"
Annette Lowman said, turning toward the back seat and speaking loudly.

Jenny gritted her teeth behind her well-practiced fake smile. *Just a
summer dream come true, to sit atop an emaciated moose and get my picture taken.*

"How much will this place cost me?" Gerald Lowman grumbled. "I
gave up a day's work for this, woman."

Jenny wanted to shout that this stupid outing had not been her idea.
Why her grandparents even bothered was beyond her. They seldom made
the trip to Sussex to see her, and when they did her grandfather either
complained or said hateful things about his son the whole time.

"You look more like him every day." Gerard Lowman gripped the steer-
ing wheel tighter, and Jennifer could see her grandfather's gritted teeth in
the rear-view mirror. The barrage of hate had begun.

"I hope to God you're nothing like him. A selfish piece of shit is what
he turned out to be. At least your mother found someone who knows how
to be a man and look after his family. But how do you think that makes
me feel, knowing some other man has to look after my granddaughter because my own son chose not to?"

"Gerry, you get yourself all wound up," Annette said, resting her hand on his shoulder. "Let's just have a good day with Jennifer. You'll get your blood pressure racing again. A nice day out will do you good. Mavis said there's lots for the young ones to do, and we'll go to the Timberland afterwards. You love their hot hamburger, dear."

Jenny chuckled to herself, thinking how the Timberland had played into both her grandmother and her mother's pep talks to sell this day. She picked up her Trixie Belden book on the seat beside her. Maybe if they saw her reading, they would stop talking. She would act excited when they got to Animal Land and smile while her grandmother took her picture. This day wouldn't last forever, and it would probably be months before they made the effort to see her again.

November 22, 2021

J enny watched the nurse pull the curtain around the bed of the other woman in the room. Miriam's loud protest outside the door made her chuckle. Two weeks ago, Jenny hadn't been too thrilled to find out that the mother of the woman she'd followed off the elevator was in the same room as her mother. But after the first few minutes, and every day since, Jenny hadn't minded at all. Miriam's visits were usually short, but she certainly was entertaining when she showed up.

"Like I haven't seen my mother's bits and pieces," Miriam Ross hollered. "But don't even worry about it. I'll stand out here and wait for you to do whatever it is you have to do. God knows I'm thrilled I don't have to wash her ass anymore. A cup of tea might be nice, but apparently boiling a kettle and putting a teabag in a cup will blow this pandemic wide open. I'll just stand out here and wait. Don't worry about me."

Jenny had been relieved to step out while the nurses attended to her mother's personal care. Each little movement seemed agonizing for her mother, and she hated hearing her moaning in pain. *Just managing her pain and discomfort* is what the doctor said earlier. *And hopefully there will be a bed for her in palliative care soon.*

But getting a bed in palliative meant someone had to die or be moved to Bobby's Hospice. The doctor had said Bobby's probably wasn't an option because her mother's time was short. When Jenny called Ryan last night, she'd tried to be gentle with that news. He'd asked if he should fly home right away, but she'd discouraged him from doing that. He'd just started a new teaching job and it seemed pointless to come just to sit at his grandmother's bedside waiting for her to die.

Rickie and Roger hadn't even mentioned coming home, and they were both short car drives, not plane trips, away. Apparently, the big sister can make all the decisions and go through the agony of watching their mother die without their help. They hadn't been any more helpful when it was Terry, and she wasn't even his daughter. She had made the arrangements to get him into the Kiwanis Nursing Home and made the weekly visits to Sussex in the two years he'd wasted away.

Miriam came back into the room carrying two coffees and a paper bag.

"I went down to Tim's. Couldn't remember how you took your coffee, so I brought creamers, milk, and sugar. Got you a doughnut, too."

"Thank you. I drink it black. Your mom is asleep."

"Thank God. I'll just drink my coffee, then slip out. Not that she even realizes I'm here or who the hell I am."

Miriam set her coffee down and unwrapped her bagel.

"You're much better at this hospital shit than I am," Miriam said. "But I don't see anybody else stepping up to take my place. There's not even any inheritance to make it worthwhile. How about you?"

"Nothing to speak of. When my stepfather went into care, Mom sold the house and moved into an apartment. My brothers helped themselves to anything of worth and left me to clean up the rest. Terry had some life insurance, but paying someone to look after Mom has pretty much depleted that."

"Aren't siblings great!" Miriam said. "Stepfather, eh? Always wished for one of those. Wished for a stepmother too, for that matter. I spent most of my childhood wishing another family would adopt me."

"That's funny, I remember wishing Farrah Fawcett Majors was my mother and that she'd show up and whisk me away to Hollywood," Jenny said. "And I used to pretend my father was Glen Campbell."

"Was your real father a musician?" Miriam asked.

"He did something in the music business. My grandmother said he went to California to make records. His name was Hank, so I'm not sure why I never imagined Hank Williams was my father. Probably because he died before I was born. I never imagined it was Hank Williams Jr., either, though. It was always Glen Campbell, even when I was more of a rock-and-roll fan."

Jenny took the doughnut from the paper bag. Taking a bite, she realized just how hungry she was. She took another bite and sip of the hot coffee before speaking.

"How did you know chocolate dip is my favourite?" Jenny asked. "My grandmother Bennett used to make the most amazing raised doughnuts and always dipped them in chocolate for me."

"You had a good grandmother, too? I never had any grandparents. Ripped off all 'round."

"I guess I'd update my mother fantasies to Betty White now," Jenny said. "But I never really wanted a different mother. My mom did the best she could with what she was given. She got pregnant in grade twelve and never graduated. I was almost two years old when my dad just up and left town."

"I wish my father had hightailed it out of the city when he knocked my mother up. We wouldn't have been any worse off, that's for sure," Miriam said.

Miriam took one last swig of coffee and chucked the cup in the garbage can. She grabbed her coat and purse from the chair, walked over to her mother's bed, and bent down to kiss her cheek.

"See you tomorrow, Jen."

1973

JD stomped up the stairs. How hard was it for them to stop calling her Jennifer Dawn? Her friends caught on right away when she'd stated she wanted to be called JD. Mom and Terry were quite happy when she dropped Lowman and started using Terry's last name, even though he hadn't adopted her. It made it easier on everyone to pretend she had the same last name as Ricky and Roger, so calling her JD was the least they could do in return.

JD slammed the door, threw her jacket on the bed, and kicked off her loafers. She'd been so excited to show her mother the album she'd bought on her trip to Saint John with Ruthie's aunt. It was her own money. God knew she'd earned every cent of it. Those Rideout brats were a handful to say the least, and fifty cents an hour looking after six kids was highway robbery. *My way or the highway,* just one of Terry's annoying sayings.

The new Mamas & the Papas album was apparently their last; they had already broken up. She had all the other ones. Her favourite was *If You Can Believe Your Ears and Eyes.* When she saw *People Like Us* in the Woolworths bin, she couldn't resist spending some of what she was saving for the bomber jacket at Zeller's. Maybe her birthday money would replace what she'd spent on the album.

Grammie and Grampie Lowman always sent her birthday cards and signed her father's name, although JD was not sure where he lived or if he was even still alive. And he probably had no idea when her birthday was or how old she was. Grammie Lowman's card selection certainly showed that her grandmother didn't realize her age. Maybe this year they'd surprise her with a more mature card, and maybe there'd be something besides a two-dollar bill inside.

November 23, 2021

"Just try it," Gloria said, passing the paintbrush to Hank. "Maybe you'll surprise yourself."

"Damn sure any creativity I have isn't at the end of a brush," Hank replied, taking the brush reluctantly. "I'll ruin your painting."

"Don't worry about that. Every painting is an experiment, and you making a couple of brushstrokes across this canvas isn't going to be the end of the world."

Hank had stopped in to see Gloria when he saw a light on. The warmth inside her small studio space was more than just respite from the elements. Every other person treated him like just another homeless bum walking the streets of uptown Saint John looking for a handout. When Gloria opened the door to welcome him in, he felt more like himself than he had in years.

"You'll be scrapping this one when I'm done with it," Hank said, dipping the brush into the powder blue paint and dabbing the top of the canvas. "Sky blue, my gran used to say about my eyes. 'Sky blue eyes on the beautiful boy.'"

"My son had blue eyes when he was born," Gloria said. "They darkened as he got older, but they were a robin's egg blue when he was a baby. I always wondered if his kids would have his beautiful eyes."

At the end of yesterday's visit, Gloria had told him about losing her oldest son. He'd been admiring the painting of the children on the beach when Gloria started crying. It had jolted him at first, and he'd almost bolted. Instead, he stayed and listened. He'd almost told her about Marvin.

"Do you think we'd ever allow ourselves to love if we had any inkling of how terrible losing them would be?" Hank asked dipping the brush again.

"I asked myself that a lot at first," Gloria said. "I remember looking at my other kids and wishing I could just run away from them. I was so

SUSAN WHITE

terrified I'd have to go through that pain again. Love is stronger than fear, though, if we allow it to be. My kids bring me such joy, and now I have grandkids. Shutting down and hiding from love would have robbed me of that. Do you have kids?"

"A daughter," Hank replied. "I did run away, out of selfishness more than fear. Thought I couldn't be me by staying. I ran from everything I had to find the life I'd dreamt about for as long as I could remember."

"Did you find it?"

Hank put the brush down and walked to the window. What had he found? He seldom let himself think about any of what California had given him. At first, he'd been proud of going after the career he ended up having. He had worked hard to get there and feeling good about that helped to quiet the guilt and confusion he felt about the choices he'd made. He'd been able to convince himself that leaving his wife and daughter and life in Saint John had been best for everyone. He would have been miserable and made everyone else miserable if he'd stayed.

"I trained as a sound engineer in California. I had an ear for mixing, balancing vocals and instruments, making quality sounding music. I was good at what I did and wouldn't change any of that." He went back to the easel and picked up the paintbrush. Painting a blue sky seemed easy enough.

"Are there parts you would change?" Gloria asked.

"Pretty obvious answer to that, since I find myself at this age with nothing to show for my work. Occasionally I stumble across an album cover with my name on it, but that doesn't buy a meal or keep me warm and dry."

Hank felt the urge to leave, afraid the emotion rising in his chest was more than he could contain. The bite in today's air would soon knock that out of him.

"I should get going," Hank said, dropping the brush back in the water.

"What's your hurry?" Gloria asked.

"I suppose I'd take another cup of tea if you're offering. Then I'll just sit here and be quiet. You aren't getting much work done gabbing to me."

"I'll put the kettle on."

As Gloria waited for the kettle to boil, she thought back to the breakfast conversation she'd had with Ted.

"What do you mean, you let a homeless guy in for tea? Are you crazy? I installed the doorbell so you could keep your doors locked, and now you're inviting them in."

"His name is Hank."

"God, woman, the next thing you'll tell me is you're letting him sleep in your studio all night."

"Would that be so bad? It seems criminal to have folks sleeping on the street when a perfectly good warm building is empty all night."

"You can't be doing that. He could burn the building down. He could bring in God knows how many others and destroy the place. You must know how stupid that would be. I know you've got a great big heart, but be serious. The homeless situation in Saint John is not your problem to fix."

"I know that. But I don't see the harm of letting the guy in to get warm and offering him a cup of tea."

Gloria came back in the room and topped up Hank's teacup.

"I sure do appreciate this, Gloria. Not many folks are as welcoming as you. Some of the stores along here don't mind if we come inside for a couple of minutes to get warm, but I don't get offered this kind of hospitality."

Gloria passed the cookies to Hank. "I don't mind at all," she said. "I enjoy chatting with you, and it's nice to take a break now and then. And how hard is it to put on a pot of tea?"

"That's what my grandmother always said, but not everyone thinks that way. Having a place where I can get warm is important, but there are a lot of other challenges to living on the street that folks probably don't think about. The rooming house I lived in wasn't great, but at least it gave me a mailing address. I was just lucky to find my October Old Age cheque, but I don't expect I'll be that lucky this month."

"Oh, no. Can you get a post office box if you don't have a permanent address? Can you even go into the post office and ask for your mail? I remember when the main post office was on Prince William Street. Seems it was easier then. I don't know if the people at Shoppers could help you or not."

"I asked the girl working at the post office desk in Brunswick Square and she was downright rude," Hank said. "She passed me a change of address card and went on to wait on the next person."

Gloria sipped her tea, considering. "You could use this address."

"I wasn't looking for that," Hank said. "My problems aren't your responsibility."

"No, I know, but there's no reason you can't use this address. We could go to Brunswick Square and fill a card out today. It won't be in time to get your November cheque sent here, but by the time your December one is issued it should come here. What do you think the people are doing with the mail that comes to your old address? Surely they're not just throwing it out."

"All the mail was in a pile of garbage and would have been thrown out if I hadn't shown up when I did. I was lucky to even get inside. They have the building locked up like Fort Knox. They couldn't care less if any of us are missing out on important mail. I took the ones I could see and gave them to the guys I managed to find. I left the other envelopes at Outflow."

"That's awful. I think if you submit a change of address form, they will redirect your mail for a period. And we can probably go online and get your government cheques directly deposited."

"I don't have a clue about computers, but having my Old Age go right to my bank account sounds good."

"I'm not that great with computers either, but I think I can help you figure that out. Are there any other places where you need to register a new mailing address?" Gloria asked.

"I suppose it wouldn't hurt to give CIBC a new address, but I can worry about that some other day," Hank replied. "Being able to use your address for now will certainly help. I really do appreciate it."

Gloria rose, picking up her cup and the empty plate. Allowing Hank to use her address seemed like the very least she could do. The tension she'd seen on his face earlier had disappeared with her suggestions and she felt glad he'd accepted her offer.

"Let's go to Lawton's right now and get your address changed," Gloria called out from the kitchen. "I told Ted I was staying late tonight anyway. How about we pick up something for supper on our way back?"

Hearing Hank's positive response, Gloria felt a flutter of hope, but it was quickly followed with the sadness of knowing that when Hank left her studio later, he'd be spending another night outdoors.

1977

"Who carries who?" Marvin asked as Hank put the key in the lock. "I suppose you should carry me over the threshold, as I'm a few pounds lighter than you."

"Can you believe it's ours?" Hank asked.

"A home of our own, thanks to my grandmother's generosity. I can only imagine how pissed off they all are that she left her money to the black sheep. Or should I say the ram who dresses as a ewe most of the time. I bet none of them expected the family disgrace to get all her money. Like the rest of them needed it. Growing potatoes for one the biggest french fry companies in the world has been pretty good for the Corbett family."

Arm in arm, Hank and Marvin made their way through the front door and over the threshold. Sun streamed in on the hardwood floors in the wide hallway.

"Well, having such a large down payment certainly made buying this house possible," Hank said. "Claiming we were just friends sharing the mortgage felt dishonest, and unfair. I'm trying to have as much faith in Harvey Milk as you do. Maybe things really will change and someday we'll be able to legally marry and have the same rights as other couples."

Marvin twirled Hank in a playful embrace before kissing him. "We have a home of our own, and we know what our love is. To hell with what anyone else thinks."

"Wish it was that easy. You go out every day and hold your head high, but I'm not blessed with your courage. At least under this roof we are free to be who we are."

"I don't know how courageous I am. I went right along with the lie, sitting there claiming you were just my friend."

Hank and Marvin walked down the long hall into the large sunny kitchen. Through the bay window the backyard looked like a separate world compared to the bustling street out front. This house on the corner of Castro and Pond Streets was right in the heart of the community they belonged to, and it was theirs. Marvin could walk to the theatre and back every night in relative safety. Hank could take the bus to and from work, his protection being the daylight and blending in.

November 23, 2021

Pearl typed in the Zoom meeting passcode and waited for the host to invite her in. Last week she hadn't said much, but just being able to say "My name is Pearl, and I'm an alcoholic" to other people again seemed worth the effort and brought her back again. She had never heard her father say those words, but somehow what he had said to her two days before he died was enough for her to grant him the forgiveness she'd not yet been able to give her mother.

"I wasn't the father you deserved, Pearl Girl."

It had taken her years to believe she deserved anything good at all, but after feeling the first glimmer of worth, she'd worked hard every day to convince herself she was not still the stupid, unlovable little girl she'd always been told she was. For years she'd believed it was her mother who stamped her heart and soul with that message. She carried that belief into a terrible marriage and into the last horrific relationship, with Carl Hayes, which had almost killed her. It wasn't until she recognized her father's rage in Carl's eyes that she realized Walter Jennings had been just as abusive as her mother.

"When you know better you do better," she heard often. She *had* known better, but it hadn't stopped her making the same mistakes with her own three kids. Mistakes that they were apparently not willing to forgive, even after Pearl's years of sobriety. Steps eight and nine had been the least successful of the twelve steps. The list was long, and trying to make amends had changed nothing.

"My name is Pearl, and I'm an alcoholic."

"Welcome, Pearl."

Pearl set the iPad down and walked across the room to grab a tissue. She stood a moment gazing out onto the street, picturing a man walking on the sidewalk, a little girl in a red coat trailing slightly behind, trying to match his long stride. Through teary eyes, she focused her gaze to the third-storey window and conjured up the image of a frail, frightened woman looking out the window watching the man and little girl walk up the street.

1977

Hank felt the sweltering heat the minute he stepped out the door. But walking along the sidewalk, he felt something else, and the first person he met gave an explanation for the quiet heaviness on the normally bustling street.

"The bastard stabbed him fifteen times. Neighbours got him to the hospital, but he didn't make it."

Hank stopped to hear details of the brutal murder of Robert Hillsborough that had taken place last night only three streets over from where he stood. For months he'd been trying to convince Marvin to be more cautious and less "out there." He begged him to dress more conservatively, to leave his flamboyant costumes in the dressing room and not wear them boldly out into the street night and day. But Marvin saw it as his mission to wear who he was proudly. Caught up in Harvey Milk's campaign, Marvin wore the button, carried the signs, and canvassed door to door, determined to make people see the injustice of the hate campaigns being waged against gay and lesbian citizens of this country.

Faggot, faggot, faggot reverberated in Hank's ears as he rushed back home. After a late-night show Marvin usually slept well into the afternoon. But he had to be the one to tell Marvin about this terrible thing, not the radio, television, or some stranger on the street. He needed to be with Marvin when he heard the horrific details of an attack that hit too close to home and to the vulnerability they both lived with every day. The killer had shouted that vile word repeatedly and then screamed, "This one's for Anita Bryant."

Who the hell would the next one be for? John Briggs, Jim Jones, Jerry Falwell? How could such hatred be justified? Robert had been a kind and gentle man living his life, harming no one. Robert and Jerry had gone out dancing, they said. Stopped for a burger. Just minding their own business and hatred targeted them. Hatred attacked them, beat Jerry, and viciously bludgeoned Robert, leaving him for dead.

Hank put his key in and turned the doorknob. Stepping into the front hall, he kicked off his shoes and headed toward the bedroom. He didn't want to startle Marvin, but he had to wake him and tell him this horrific news as gently as possible. Hank couldn't go about his business as if nothing had happened. He couldn't just go to work, sit down at the board, and move dials and knobs all day. He needed to hold Marvin and they needed to weep together for Robert, for Jerry, and for each other.

The shrill ring of the telephone stopped him just as he got to the bedroom door. He rushed back to the living room and grabbed the receiver.

"Where the hell are you, Lowman? Glen Campbell's session is at ten and we need to be set up. Time is money, asshole."

November 24, 2021

H ank stopped partway up King Street, turning out of the wind to catch his breath. He still had the gift card tucked into his parka pocket, and getting out of the cold air would be welcome. He felt out of sorts today. Lonelier than usual and more irritable.

Staring down the hill toward the harbour, Hank could see the Canadian flag waving in front of city hall. *Canada.* Marvin had never called him anything else. The first morning they'd spent together had been the beginning of something Hank had never imagined he would be given. They'd sat at Jerry's Diner for hours. In a strange California city, he had found another little New Brunswick boy who had grown up feeling just as out of place.

"My grammie used to quote a verse in the Bible to me," Marvin said that morning.

Hank closed his eyes and could hear Marvin's voice reciting the words like a mantra he held close: "I praise you because I am fearfully and wonderfully made; your works are wonderful; I know that full well."

"Grammie said God doesn't make mistakes, Canada." Hank had taken those words into his soul as he mustered the courage to see himself honestly and allowed himself to fall in love with Marvin.

"Hank, you going in?"

Startled back to the present, Hank turned to see Pearl approaching. "Yeah. My treat," he called out.

1977

"He won his seat!" Marvin shouted. "I told you Harvey would do it. You know, this is just the start of the changes the Mayor of Castro will bring about for us."

"If they let him live," Hank replied.

"I am putting on my glitziest ensemble and strutting down to city hall carrying an *I Voted for Harvey Milk* sign. Nothing's going to change if we don't stick together and make a little noise."

"Well, you go ahead. I have a day job to get to. I'll celebrate in my own way. No high heels and big wigs for me."

"Boring, but that's why I love you, Canada. Not everyone can pull off Mae West on a Monday morning."

"Well then, let's both go do what we do," Hank said, grabbing his jacket off the hall tree. "But you be careful," Hank added before kissing Marvin goodbye and running out the door.

November 25, 2021

*G*loria flipped the sign on the door to *Open*, pulled up the blinds, filled the kettle, and turned the radio on to catch the CBC eight o'clock news.

Two young brothers dead in a single-vehicle crash. The words hit her in the gut. The announcer spoke the headline in a monotone voice, holding no trace of the misery that accompanied the actual event. Someone had just been told their two sons were dead. Today a family was facing an unimaginable loss that would forever be a marker between before and after.

Gloria went to the door and flipped the *Open* sign to *Closed*. She slumped to the couch as her mind took her back to the nightmare of those first hours.

Of course, right away they had had to go through all the rituals a death requires. Funeral arrangements, choosing a casket, dictating an obituary. Gloria recalled grabbing notepaper to jot down a hurried list of Zac's friends for pallbearers. Newscasts don't tell of that misery. Or the torture of waiting for your youngest son to wake up so that you can rush to him before he hears the commotion downstairs or quietly stumbles into the chaotic frenzy of...of what?

They'd driven back home to several cars already in the yard that morning, and there'd been a steady stream of people in and out all day. Food started arriving and kept coming for a full month afterwards. What generosity is shown at first. The families affected by today's news clip would no doubt receive that too. It's in the months and years after a loss that grief becomes a more solitary journey. Life goes on, but yours is never the same.

At first, she had sobbed almost hourly, then daily, and then somehow, as time passed, less often as the pain somehow became more manageable. But sometimes the floodgates opened and returned in a deluge. When the sobbing came it felt the same as it did in those first days, the panic just as intense. Gloria lowered her head and gave in to it.

The sound of loud knocking on the windowpane behind her stopped the sobbing short and Gloria turned her head to look out. The hood of the parka was tied tight around the man's face, but she recognized Hank, his blue eyes showing through heavy eyebrows, his whiskers frosty and white. His knocking continued as he brought his face closer to the glass. Gloria stood and walked into the hall, unlocked, and opened the door, motioning for Hank to come in.

"Lock the door behind you, would you please? I am not open for business."

"I can see that," Hank said. He gently led Gloria back into her studio. His eyes filled with tears as his voice faltered. "Are you all right?"

"Right as rain. Peachy keen. Just fine." Gloria sat back down on the couch, grabbed a Kleenex, and dabbed at her sodden cheeks.

"That's what fine looks like, is it?" Hank said. "Mind if I put the kettle on? Looks like you could use a cuppa."

"Always the cure. Absolutely. I've got some biscuits out there too. Tea and crumpets, just the ticket."

Gloria lowered her head into her hands, feeling the exhaustion that intense emotion brings. Hearing Hank in the kitchen, she felt the comfort of his presence.

Hank returned to the studio a few minutes later with two steaming cups of tea and a plate of buttered and jammed biscuits.

"The only thing missing is the clotted cream," Hank said, setting the tray down. He pulled up a chair and sat across from Gloria. "Have a couple of sips, then tell me what's put you in a funk this morning."

"A funk. Now that's a damn fine word for it."

"I expected to see you at the easel when I walked by," Hank said. "Thought maybe your *Closed* sign was on account of a deadline or something. Or maybe too absorbed in your art to open up. Glad I bothered looking in."

Gloria steadied her tea cup in her hands. "Thanks, Hank."

SUSAN WHITE

"Do you want to talk about it?"

"I'm no stranger to crying," Gloria said slowly, almost dismissively, not sure she was up to sharing more than that. She took a sip of the tea and reached for another tissue, dabbing at the tears on her cheek. "It's always right there, you know," she continued. "It's no shock when it boils up and the tears come. More shocking to me is how I can go so long without crying."

"It can be a hard slog," Hank said, passing Gloria the plate of biscuits. "Grief is a brutal companion by times, but it's the price we pay to love."

Gloria took a small bite of the biscuit, unsure she could chew and swallow. She processed Hank's words and raised her head to look more closely at his face, those blue eyes still the focal point. In those eyes she saw compassion, understanding, and a familiar sadness.

"What's the loss you carry, Hank?"

"How do you know I've lost someone?"

"I see it in your eyes. Plus, you don't get to be our age without loss. Your parents are both dead, I assume."

"Yeah, but I lost them long before they passed away." Hank stood up, teacup in hand, and moved toward the window. "Not sure I ever had them, truth be told. They never knew me, that's for damn sure. I left Saint John when I was nineteen and I think they decided then I was dead as far they were concerned."

"As a mother, I doubt that, Hank."

Hank cleared his throat and walked back into the kitchen.

1978

"We're going, Canada," Marvin hollered from the other room. "Harvey gets sworn in today, and we are going to be there."

"And you're wearing that?" Hank asked, walking into the bedroom.

"You are such a killjoy," Marvin said. "My boy Harvey says we'll never win our rights by staying quietly in the closet."

"I get that, but do you have to wear the glitziest thing *in* your closet? Can't you just carry a sign or wear a button like the rest of us?"

"I'm not afraid to strut my stuff and shout out loud exactly who I am. You've got to stop being so afraid, Canada. Harvey Milk is an elected official, a city and county supervisor. He's going to get Prop 6 defeated, and that'll just be the start of the change he's going to bring to this city, the state of California, and the whole damn country. None of that change will come from hiding who we are. Fly our flag, Gilbert says."

November 25, 2021

*L*iam hurried across the square to Service NB. Hopefully the lineup wouldn't be long and he could get his vehicle registration updated with his current address. Work was slow today, so even if he took more than his lunch hour it would be no big deal. He'd get in and out as quickly as possible, though, and with any luck run into Hank and spend some time with him.

Hank had been on his mind a lot the last few days. The temperature had really dropped, and Liam wasn't sure where Hank was living. Every time he asked him, Hank changed the subject, which seemed like a clear indication he had no permanent address.

Leaving Service NB, Liam spotted Hank crossing King's Square and walked to meet him.

"Well, hello, young fella," Hank said as he turned to see Liam approaching. "I was on our bench waiting for you, but when you didn't show I figured you must have been too busy to take your lunch break today."

"I had something to take care of first. Nothing packed for my lunch today. Amanda was too busy and I was in a hurry to get going this morning. Thought I'd run over to the market and buy my lunch. Can I get you something while I'm at it?"

"No need of that. I had tea and biscuits with a friend a bit ago. And they're serving supper at Stone Church tonight."

"Well, that's nice, but I don't think a sandwich will spoil your appetite. I'm getting a grilled chicken wrap and a coffee. Okay if I get you the same?"

"Well, if you insist," Hank said. "My treat next time. We mustn't have that wife of yours thinking you've got another mouth to feed. Can't be easy making ends meet these days."

"I'll leave you my phone. Thought we might listen to some Mamas & the Papas today. Since our last chat I've become a bit obsessed with their career trajectory. Do you remember how to search?"

"You're not afraid I'll run off with your phone and try to get a few bucks for it?"

Liam rolled his eyes and passed Hank his phone. "Milk and sugar?"

"I like cream, but beggars shouldn't be choosers."

"Well then, cream it is. I'll get you one of their butter tart squares too. We'll have a party."

1978

There's a pot of gold at the end of the rainbow, thought Hank as he and Marvin rounded the corner onto Castro Street. Gran always told him that someday he'd find his pot of gold at the end of the rainbow.

For weeks, Marvin along with several other volunteers had helped the drag queen Gilbert Baker fashion the flag that would lead this year's June march to celebrate Gay Freedom Day. They had gathered on the roof of the gay community centre to dip fabric into big barrels of dye. The fabric was cut and sewn together, creating a huge flag of eight colourful strips, each representing a message of hope and change to resonate through the streets of this city and spread out through this country and beyond. The community had quickly embraced the flag's design and message, duplicating it on signs and banners.

Would people like John Briggs, Anita Bryant, and Jerry Falwell continue to spew hatred and disgust if this flag was flown everywhere? Would change come when fifteen million gay men and women across this country pushed their way out of the closet?

Gilbert Baker had grown up in a small town in Kansas, and like so many others, had kept who he really was hidden from friends and family. Many gay men had chosen paths they hoped would help them blend in and conform to what was expected of them. Gilbert had joined the US army; Hank had married Tanya. Marvin had been braver from the start, but he'd been disowned by his parents and community. Still, Gilbert, Marvin, and Hank had each found their way to San Francisco and to an acceptance of their own sexuality. Hank knew that not everyone was as fortunate.

Had George ever felt that acceptance? Had he even been able to truly accept himself? It seemed as if George had chosen an isolated island and the life of a lobster fisherman as a way to escape. Hank choked back the guilt he always felt when thinking about George. Would things have been different if he'd been brave enough to tell George how much he loved him long before he did?

Marvin reached for Hank's hand as they picked up the pace to join the already large crowd. What a different vibe on the street this morning compared to a year ago, when they'd gathered for Robert Hillsborough's funeral procession. Was this the change Marvin always spoke of?

"Hope and love will conquer fear and hatred, Canada," Marvin shouted as the cacophony of excited voices grew around them.

Hank thought back to the newscast he'd watched last night showing Jerry Falwell speaking to a large crowd, loudly declaring a war on homosexuality. Would men like Robert still be targeted and murdered? Would the Thomas Spooners and John Cordovas of this world still carry out such horrific attacks? Would little boys and girls still grow up hiding who they were and who they loved?

Hank felt the breeze and the strong sunshine. He looked toward the maze of bodies and colour and took in the exuberance of the crowd. Chants of courage, determination, and hope echoed all around. Music and dancing, swaying bodies, and outward displays of love and affection between same-sex couples made up this bubbling, burgeoning crowd. The gathering felt alive with possibility and hope, and today he would embrace that hope.

Flanked by hundreds, Marvin and Hank turned off Castro Street, joining thousands more with signs and banners waving, and floats and marching bands merging to build the momentum of this year's Gay Freedom Parade.

Gilbert's rainbow flag streamed out behind Harvey Milk, who was leading the throng.

"I am Harvey Milk, and I am here to recruit you. You must come out!" Harvey shouted through the megaphone. "Hope cannot be silent!"

November 30, 2021

Miriam Ross shoved some of her mother's things into a plastic bag. Minutes earlier she'd watched her mother take a laboured breath in. No exhale followed. Who knew it was that abrupt? Here one minute and gone the next. The relief that followed was staggering and caused a flood of emotion Miriam hadn't been expecting. Of course, the nurse who witnessed it chalked it up to a normal show of grief, and Miriam did not correct her.

This charade was over. She didn't have to come back to this room and play the part of the doting daughter. Taking her leave so quickly had been the most unselfish, unceremonious act her mother had ever performed. Now Miriam was off the hook, the last detail being to clear the room of her mother's possessions and throw the bag away. No loose ends. Only emotional clutter left to deal with, and she'd perfected that art a long time ago.

Inventing a more desired past and playacting a perfect present were her main resources for dealing with having grown up with a drunken, abusive father, a weak and spineless mother, and the low bar they'd both set for her. Mary MacAllister no longer existed, and now there was no one left to drag her back to the childhood she'd worked so hard to forget.

Even the funeral arrangements had been tailored to be efficient, requiring no pretense of the grieving daughter. No viewing, no service; just cremation and closure. She owed no explanation to siblings who had flown the coop early and made a point of staying as far away as possible. She'd email them and have the funeral home send copies of the death certificate.

"Are you okay?" Jenny asked, entering the room. "The nurse told me your mother passed."

"You startled me. Yes, I'm fine. They kept her pretty drugged up. She was in no pain and the end came quickly. How is your mom doing?"

"Pretty doped up too. I don't think she even knows when I'm here now, but it doesn't seem right leaving her alone for very long. I was outside for a bit of fresh air and the nurse told me about your mom on my way by. I'm glad I caught you before you left. Are you sure you're all right?"

Miriam pulled open the drawer of the metal table beside the bed and threw the items in on top of the rest before tying up the plastic bag. She'd chuck it in the dumpster when she got to the parking lot. "The hardest part of all this is not looking too happy," she said. "Don't suppose they see many people leaving this floor doing a dance of joy."

Miriam set the plastic bag on floor and sat down abruptly. The frenzy she'd worked herself into in the last few minutes was catching up with her and she felt a wave of nausea.

"I must sound pretty heartless to you," Miriam said. "I bet you're glad to see the end of me."

"I was thinking the exact opposite, actually," Jenny said. "Why don't we go downstairs and have a coffee? How about a chocolate-dipped doughnut to celebrate your release?"

"Sounds like a plan," Miriam answered.

1978

"Oh my god!" Marvin screamed. "Harvey's dead."

Hank rushed into the living room. Marvin was standing in front of the television screen, his face pained with shock and disbelief as the newscaster gave details of the two murders in San Francisco City Hall.

"He shot Mayor Moscone first," Marvin exclaimed. "Then he went down the hall and found Harvey. How can this be happening?"

"Have they said who shot them?" Hank asked.

"Feinstein is saying it was Dan White," Marvin answered pacing back and forth in front of the television. "Harvey is dead. Harvey is dead. Oh my god, I can't believe this."

Hank thought back to the speech he and Marvin had heard Harvey give just a few days ago after months of death threats, bomb threats, even bombs sent directly to him in City Hall. Security had been increased, with locked doors, armed guards, and metal detectors in place.

Harvey had spoken to the receptive crowd with such conviction and bravery. Hank crumpled to a chair, fully realizing that the heinous prediction in Harvey's directive had actually come about.

If a bullet should enter my brain, let that bullet destroy every closet door.

December 2, 2021

Miriam Ross slowed as she walked toward the art studio. The client she'd gifted the beach painting to had been very impressed. With a couple more sales pending in the Kennebecasis area, it might be a good idea to stock up. The artist also had some nice uptown paintings that would be suitable for clients buying in the southern peninsula, a hot commodity these days. It would be helpful to be known as the generous realtor who gave nice closing gifts and supported local talent.

As Miriam stepped up to ring the bell, an old, scruffy, bearded man in a discoloured parka opened the door and stepped out onto the sidewalk. She gave him a wide berth. No doubt the cold air lessened the smell she was sure this man would give off in a closer, more confined space. Hopefully she wouldn't be hit with the lingering odour when she entered the building.

"Bye, Hank. Come by and you can finish your painting tomorrow."

"Giving art lessons to the down and out now, are you?" Miriam asked as she stepped into the entryway. "Aren't you kindhearted?"

Gloria ushered Miriam into the studio motioning toward an easel in the corner. "Hank is a friend, but he's also a talented artist. He's almost finished this painting of a fishing boat. I think it's amazing. You can almost feel the heavy fog and taste the salt air."

Miriam scrunched her nose and gave a dismissive grunt. "I guess that's why you're the artist and I sell real estate. Just looks like a decrepit, worthless old boat to me."

"What can I help you with today?" Gloria asked.

"I bought one of your little beach prints a while ago. I'm looking for a couple more and some of your city ones. They make lovely little thank you gifts for my clients. You can give me a receipt for tax purposes, right?"

"Oh yes, for sure. I'll let you have a look while I clean up a bit. I need to close at four today. My granddaughter is in her school play tonight."

Miriam watched Gloria pick up the teacups and dishes from the small table by the window. She wasn't just teaching the man to paint; it looked as if she was feeding him as well.

"Is that man homeless? I hope you're not being taken advantage of." Miriam raised her voice as Gloria walked out of the room. "They cannot be trusted, you know. I had a client who let one sleep in her garden shed, and at first it seemed harmless enough. Then he started bringing more men by, and she was broken into last month. She couldn't prove it was one of the men who'd been sleeping in her shed, but it doesn't take a genius to figure it out. Give them an inch and they'll take a mile. You cannot be too cautious." She paced a bit. Keeping a potential customer waiting seemed rude. "I'm interested in making a purchase," Miriam hollered in to the next room.

A few seconds later Gloria returned, picked up the water jar, took it to the sink, and began cleaning the paintbrushes. Miriam walked across the room, feeling the colour rise in her face.

"I want ten beach prints if you have them, and five city prints," Miriam said loudly. "I've got to scoot. Could you bag each one up in your lovely little gift bags for me? I'll come by in a few days and pick them up."

1979

H ank jolted awake, his mind cloudy, remembering he and Marvin in the middle of the huge swell of bodies that descended on city hall on November 27, the day of the murders. The numbers grew to the thousands as they marched in solidarity to city hall. The march even in its magnitude remained peaceful, respectful, and quietly reverent. It was a gathering of mourners, each horrified, saddened, and shocked by the two brutal murders that had been committed that day. Each person marching seemed to be carrying the heavy burden of that reality, alongside the hurts and hatred they themselves had endured. The actions that had taken the lives of two strong and passionate men felt like the very acts of hatred and violence each person there had experienced, but the crowd focused on the tragedy and stayed peaceful out of respect for the two slain men.

The six months since then had been a blur of rage, disbelief, and fear. They had tried so hard to hang on to shards of hope as Dan White's trial unfolded. Surely the deliberate and vicious act of taking two lives would not go unpunished, they'd thought. How wrong they had been. But who could have predicted the nightmare they were living through now?

Hank shifted his position, reaching out for Marvin's hand, being careful not to disturb the tangle of tubes and connections coming from both sides of Marvin's hospital bed. From the start, the march last night had been totally the opposite of the one in November. Anger, disbelief, and utter indignation for the verdict delivered yesterday fuelled an uproar that quickly became an inferno. *Manslaughter*, a claim that Dan White's actions were not premeditated, but brought on by depression, possibly a lack of sleep or a poor diet. Every word and each syllable of that verdict sank deep into the heart of each man and woman who descended on City Hall.

By nightfall the march was a lethal mix of chaos, violence, and destruction. Protestors smashed windows in the nearby buildings and in parked cars. The boiling crowd broke through police barriers to ram the doors of City Hall. Beatings and attacks left hundreds injured on both sides of the protest. Instead of candles flickering in calm tribute, rows of burning police cars blazed into the raging night.

Marvin and Hank had been there at the beginning, but sensing the rising anger and the erupting volatility, Hank had begged Marvin to retreat, and surprisingly Marvin had consented. They had hurried home to the sanctuary of their Pond Street home, both hunkering down until Marvin left to do his midnight show.

"If only I'd convinced you to *stay* home," Hank muttered, leaning over and kissing Marvin's cheek.

Hank had rushed to the hospital after getting a call from the club saying Marvin had been taken to Saint Francis by ambulance, his condition unknown. He'd been given few details of the attack, but in the first few hours all he'd cared about was that Marvin was still alive.

From piecing together fragments, Hank believed the attacks began around one o'clock in the morning. Marvin had just finished his set when several police officers dragged him out of his dressing room and began beating him. Other officers were systematically attacking any patrons still in the theatre, shouting threats of revenge and retribution at the already traumatized men and women, most of whom had endured the riots and made their way to the club for some reprieve and safety.

When the terror was over, several victims were badly injured, with Marvin among the worst of them. The officers who had targeted him had taken perverse pleasure in degrading and humiliating the man hidden beneath a shimmering golden gown, jewels, and a blazing red wig.

Hank startled as the door opened.

"Mr. Lowman? I'm Dr. Randall. Are you a relative of Mr. Corbett's?"

Hank gripped Marvin's hand harder. He'd been waiting for this question. Up until now the nurses had tolerated his presence and even been kind, but he'd not been asked anything about his relationship to the patient.

"Mr. Corbett is my husband," Hank declared, loudly rising to his feet.

Dr. Randall approached and placed a hand on Hank's quivering shoulder.

"I don't give a shit what the law says," Hank continued. "Marvin is my husband."

"Well, we'll work around those details," Dr. Randall replied calmly. "If Mr. Corbett has no other relatives nearby, you could be declared his guardian. Is there anyone you could contact to give you written permission for that?"

"No one. He hasn't had any contact with his family for at least ten years. I'm all he has. I don't give a damn what the law says. Men who supposedly uphold the law are the ones who nearly killed him. You will need to call them to drag me out of here. I am not leaving Marvin's side."

"How about we start again, Mr. Lowman?" Dr. Randall said. "Sit down and take a deep breath."

Dr. Randall pulled up a stool. He set the clipboard down on the end of the bed and waited for Hank to regain his composure. "What I've come to tell you is not good news. I am afraid the attack has left Mr. Corbett completely paralyzed on one side, with very little mobility on the other. And we will not know the extent of damage to his brain until the swelling goes down."

Hank gasped, swiping at the tears streaming down his cheeks.

Dr. Randall stood, grabbed a box of tissues, and passed it to Hank. "Mr. Corbett has a long recovery ahead and we will do whatever we can. But we know for certain he will need a lot of care." He leaned forward. "The nurses tell me you haven't left his side, and that's good enough for me. I don't care if you and Mr. Corbett are legally registered in the California registry of marriages or not. As far as I'm concerned, you will be told everything, and if any decisions need to be made, we'll figure that out later."

December 3, 2021

Hank had been tossing and turning since settling into his sleeping bag. The tarp overhead kept flapping, and Hank expected the next strong gust of wind would lift it off completely. The tarp did not provide much shelter, but it kept the rain off. If it ended up flying across the causeway and into open water, there would be no getting it back.

Hank had built the enclosure well down the rock-covered bank, hoping the slope would provide a wind break and help Hank stay hidden from the causeway traffic. When he walked toward the causeway there was only one spot where he could see the blue tarp. The fact it had been undisturbed for almost a month seemed to validate his choice of location.

It was a nasty night. The wind and snow blew briskly as he'd walked home along Union Street. The folks at Stone Church had served up a hearty supper and there had been lots of hot tea and sweets. On account of the bad weather, they were letting some stay the night, but he'd been worried about his tarp. He wanted to make sure the corners were secure and be there if it started to blow off so he could refasten it and protect his few possessions.

So far no one had bothered any of his things. He'd heard horror stories on the street about deliberate vandalism and theft. Not that he had anything worth stealing. It just seemed sometimes the most miserable people wanted others to be more miserable than they were. Hank had managed to stay under the radar and pretty much keep to himself. It helped that he had no drugs or alcohol to steal.

Hank turned again and pulled his sleeping bag up over his head. He had survived harder nights, and lying here waiting for the worst wouldn't change anything. If tonight's storm demolished his makeshift home, he'd do what he'd done countless times. He would do whatever he needed to just keep going, even though most days he wasn't sure why he bothered.

1980

Standing in line in this crowded, windowless room was making Hank's head spin. Did every government office have to be such a drab, impersonal space? And did every employee have to be so heartless? Earlier he'd waited almost an hour to get to the front of the line, only to be told he didn't have the right paperwork to register Marvin for his disability allowance.

Hank had taken the bus home to get the medical form required. Patsy could only stay another two hours with Marvin, so Hank had rushed out the door and caught the bus back. He'd be lucky if he reached the front of the line before the woman pulled down the screen and closed her wicket. And if he fainted, would anyone let him back in his spot once he came to? He may as well just call it off and admit this entire exercise had been a waste of time.

He hated to have to tell Marvin he'd failed at getting his claim submitted. He'd hoped to cheer him up with that at least, as little else brought any joy to Marvin these days. Hank tried to be as patient and understanding as he could, but there were times he wanted to shut the front door and just run away.

He would never do that, of course.

He staggered a bit as the line moved ahead.

"Are you all right?"

Hank turned to respond to the lady behind him. At first glance she reminded him of his grandmother. Her kind face and caring words brought a lump to Hank's throat. When was the last time anyone had asked him if he was all right? After the attack, people had been outraged and sympathetic. Protests had been organized to voice that outrage and anger, but soon even the support of close friends had fizzled when they were faced with the stark reality of Marvin's injuries. That night had impacted so many, and the entire community was suffering.

"These lines are brutal, aren't they?" Hank said. "I just get a bit dizzy standing so long. I'm not complaining. I see the poor buggers wheeling up here waiting in line with the rest of us. Should be a better system. Most of those guys fought for their country and this is what they get."

"That's the truth. Some days I thank the good lord it's just old age and bad choices that put me here. And I don't suppose I have too much longer on this side of the sod. What kick in the pants brings you here?"

"I'm filing for a friend," Hank answered.

"Is he a veteran?"

Hank felt his eyes well up, emotion and rage swelling the lump he was attempting to swallow. He seldom put into words the impact of what had happened eight months ago, and telling this woman seemed implausible, yet words spilled out of his mouth.

"Not of Vietnam. A different war that nearly killed him and a battle that left him for dead. There are times we both think death would have been easier."

"God love you, son. He is lucky to have you. What's your man's name?"

"Marvin. Marvin Corbett. He'd be my husband if that right were afforded us. Thank you for asking."

December 3, 2021

Sitting by the window in the Uptown Eatery, Miriam saw Jenny's car pull into an empty spot right outside. Since their Tim Horton's date on the day Miriam's mother died, Miriam and Jenny had been trying to meet for lunch. Both were unwilling to let go of the friendship that had grown sitting together in that hospital room, but Miriam was busy with work, and Jenny was still sitting vigil at her mother's bedside.

"Have you been here long?" Jenny asked, slipping into the seat across the table from Miriam. "I had to wait to speak to the doctor before I could get away."

"Any change?" Miriam asked.

"They're going to put her in Bobby's Hospice as soon as a room comes available. I hate the fact that someone has to die for Mom to go there."

"It will be a nicer place for her and for you, Jen."

"I know. But part of me just wishes she'd slip away in the night, be gone when I come in the morning, and that none of this next part would be necessary. I know that sounds terrible."

"Do you forget who you're talking to?" Miriam asked. "I understand completely. At least you love your mother and will miss her. Does Ryan plan on coming home anytime soon?"

"He and Serge will come for the funeral, but Ryan wants to see her before she dies. He's coming next Friday, just for the weekend. I'm trying to discourage him; Mom won't even realize he's there, and I'd rather he remember her the way she was instead of how she is now. But he's made up his mind and already booked his flight. God, my brothers live a lot closer, and they make no effort to come."

"Family is funny, isn't it? My sister keeps calling me asking and me where certain things are. Ridiculous things, like my mother's crystal candy dish. I don't even remember her having anything crystal. Apparently, she used to fill it with Chicken Bones at Christmas time. And she wants the platter Mom used to put the turkey on. Funny how sisters growing up in the same house have such different memories. I do not remember Mom having anything nice, and I certainly don't have warm and cozy Christmas memories."

"My brothers took a lot of stuff after Terry died," Jenny said. "Then Mom moved into a small apartment, so I have very little to dispose of. You don't have any of your mother's things, do you? Doesn't your sister know that?"

"Yes, but somehow she's convinced herself we're a normal family with heirlooms and treasures to pass on instead of a shitload of dysfunction."

"I've been thinking a lot about my father lately," Jenny said. "When I was growing up, I pretended he didn't matter. In my early twenties I went through a stage when I got a bit obsessed with finding out whatever I could about him. Then I just let on that he was dead as it seemed easier. But now I can't seem to shake the longing I feel to find him and know him before it's too late. That probably sounds dumb to you."

"Not dumb at all," Miriam said. "My father deserved to be written off and forgotten. He didn't run away for real, but he sure as hell didn't show up in any meaningful way. But you never got to know your father, so it makes sense to wonder about him."

"Did I tell you how much Ryan looks like my dad? I grabbed a photograph of my father in his teens off the board at my grandmother's funeral. As Ryan got older it shocked me how much they look alike."

"Yes. DNA is strong," Miriam said. "I use a lot of makeup and hair dye to keep from seeing my mother every time I look in the mirror."

"My grandmother used to say I had my father's eyes and his curly hair. My grandfather said I had his stubborn streak but never meant it in a nice way."

"Like I say, family, isn't it great?"

Miriam and Jenny gave the server their lunch order and passed her the menus.

"I used to be so angry that my father never tried to find me, but the older I get the more I mellow," Jenny said, taking a swig of her ice water.

"Age doesn't seem to be mellowing me, but I'm glad you aren't holding on to the anger and hurt. It's not the best way to go through life."

"I don't know how I'd go about finding out if my father is still alive. I don't think there are any other relatives still living. I don't even know if he still lives in California. He sent flowers when his mother died. If I was a detective on a TV show, I'd track down the flower shop and get his address."

"Real life is no TV show. What's your father's name?"

"Henry Vincent Lowman is the name on my birth certificate. Mom always called him Hank."

"Hank Lowman. Okay. I'll keep my ears open. Maybe you and I will end up being like Cagney and Lacey, and find him."

1980

Jenny Davis set the albums she'd selected down on the counter. The cashier looked up and stopped sorting through the box of albums someone had just dropped off. This was Jenny's first time into Backstreet Records, and she had spent over an hour leafing through the wide selection of albums. The owner had met her at the door, quickly starting up a mostly one-sided conversation.

"My name's Gordie, Gordie Tufts. This place is a passion of mine. But we've got a damn good selection of some of the best music ever released on vinyl. Anything I can help you find today?"

It would seem so stupid to say she just wanted to look at albums recorded in California. Saying that she was searching specifically for albums listing Hank Lowman as the sound engineer would be even more ridiculous.

"I'm doing a bit of research," Jenny finally offered. "It's a design course I'm taking. Looking at record jackets mostly, not really for a specific band or artist. Maybe I'll start with artists recording in California."

"Take your time. Album covers are works of art. They tell a story in themselves and often reveal a lot about the musicians they are created for. I'll be out back, but if you find some treasures you can't live without, Patty will be happy to take your money. Reasonable prices here, too. Not in it for the money, my wife would probably tell you."

Jenny started with the Beach Boys, the Byrds, Crosby, Stills &Nash, then Three Dog Night. On the back of the second Grateful Dead album, she found the name Hank Lowman. Actually seeing her father's name brought more emotion than she anticipated. The truth was, she really hadn't expected to find it. Had she even believed her father had the career in the music business? Scanning several Mama & the Papas album jackets, she discovered her father's name listed in the credits on two of their albums. It was so weird that these were two she hadn't collected in her teens.

"Good choice, the Dead and the Mamas & the Papas. A music aficionado, are you?" the cashier said.

"It's kind of in my blood, I guess," Jenny said, offering no more than that.

December 3, 2021

Pearl woke shaking and disoriented. In the dream he'd been standing over her, and the terror had been as real as all the times when something escalated and brought out the violence in him. The man who surfaced in those moments was nothing like the gentle, caring man she'd been attracted to the very first day they met in Queen Square. It was his eyes she'd noticed first, large blue orbs with staggering depth and clarity.

Staggering seemed like a fitting description for those days, but Pearl hadn't been too drunk to take notice of the man sitting on the bench across from her and even found the nerve to strike up a conversation. She had been careful to weigh each word, as breaking into one of her tirades would likely send him hightailing it out of the square. She had that effect on most people. The crazy, drunk bag lady, the most common descriptor. Not many people took the time to chat to her. But Carl had.

"Lovely day, isn't it?" Pearl said.

"I love watching the buds bursting on the branches of these beautiful old deciduous trees," Carl said. "I could sit here all day long. Mind if I join you? Before long the leaves will be green and full and these beauties will offer shade all summer. There's not a place in this grand old city I love more than right here. Our forebears were some generous to have planted these trees and built this square for our enjoyment. Seems the least we can do is appreciate the beauty. Do you come here often?"

For several days in a row, she had gone to Queen Square hoping to see the blue-eyed man with all the fancy words and ideas again. On the fifth day he was there, exactly where she'd seen him the first time. He'd come right over and bowed to her as if addressing royalty.

"Well, here's the lovely lady I've been waiting for."

Carl was a charmer, and after a few more meetings in Queen Square, Pearl invited him to move in to her small apartment on Wentworth Street.

It took nearly two years to be rid of him. But as brutal as he was, the misery he inflicted was the catalyst she'd needed to get sober.

Pearl got out of bed and walked out into the kitchen, determined to bring herself back to the present. She was safe in the small second-storey apartment she'd moved into seven years ago. She took comfort in the security of being alone behind two locked doors, and since moving in, she'd never allowed anyone to come inside.

1982

Hank ran the bath as hot as he could stand before lowering himself into the tub. This gaudy pink bathtub had given Marvin such pleasure. Hank preferred to shower and never took full advantage of the bathtub's roomy shell-shaped design. After the attack, Marvin was unable to use the bathtub or the shower, depending on Hank to wash and groom him. The tub then became a place of escape for Hank.

He hadn't allowed himself that luxury in the days following Marvin's death. Going through the motions, he'd quickly showered and carried on— except for the day of the funeral. That morning he'd run a bath and gotten in, even though it seemed self-indulgent. He'd added hot water twice, stalling the inevitable. He had to get out, get dressed, and make his way to Duggan's in time for the service. And of course, he'd gotten out.

Hank wasn't so sure today. He'd set the alarm to get up for his first day back to work and jumped up when he heard it go off. He'd gone into the kitchen, made the coffee, and run his bath. His body was going through the motions, but his brain was doing the opposite.

Could he immerse himself fully into the water and keep his head under long enough? What if he just stayed in the water and succumbed to eventual hypothermia? How long would it be before anyone came looking to see why he hadn't shown up for work, or why they hadn't seen him at the market or out and about in days? Who would be the one to find him?

::

Hank's eyes whipped open. He quickly focused, attempting to quiet the terror of the dream. He could see the sliver of light under the door. It was never completely dark in here, and never completely quiet. The noise of the staff moving about, the fluorescent lights, and the outbursts of patients seemed to permeate every hour, and he'd not had a peaceful night since being admitted.

He recalled the loud banging on the bathroom door, but nothing past that. And it had been a few days before he even realized where he was. The medication was keeping him groggy and lethargic, only waking to his own or another's outburst of terror.

Hank rolled over and pulled the rigid blankets up over his face. The dream had seemed so real. He'd been standing on the deck watching as George was swallowed up by huge waves of dark water. Before sinking the final time, George had clutched at the string around his neck. As his head bobbed up one last time, the terrified face was Marvin's. The water quickly calmed and each pearl fell away, bouncing over the waves like the stones Hank used to skip on Tin Can Beach.

December 6, 2021

H ank sat on a bench looking over at the crowd gathering in the square. A protest of some kind was forming, and Hank could feel tension in the cold air. The police contingent was increasing as well, leading Hank to believe authorities thought whatever was brewing might not stay peaceful. He'd already been asked to move by a police officer and had complied immediately, but sitting here now he could feel his anxiety rising. Large crowds and police presence had a way of doing that to him, even though he knew the threat was nothing like the days that followed the Dan White verdict.

Hank looked up and saw Bruce walking toward him. "Bunch of crazies filling the square," he said. "Anti-vaxxers. There's a crowd marching on city hall, and word is they plan to block King Street. Don't know what they think the mayor is going to do. All these COVID restrictions are provincial or federal. But the cops are getting antsy. One officer just asked me if you were trouble."

"Right, like an old man sitting on a bench minding his own business is a threat?" Hank said. "I've got my vaccinations, and my protest days are long over."

"Want me to get you away from this mess?" Bruce asked. "How about we head over west and have lunch at AJ's? Best I get the city truck out of here anyway, if they start throwing stuff or, God forbid, burning vehicles like back in the day when protests got ugly."

Hank started walking with Bruce, happy to take him up on his offer. He could tell this guy a thing or two about the difference between peaceful and violent protests; a candlelight vigil compared to the White Night Riots. But he kept silent.

::

"Can I drive you home?" Bruce asked as he and Hank walked out of AJ's Restaurant.

"Home, now ain't that a nice thought? I owned a house once, you know, in San Francisco, and we were lucky to get it when we did. Prices climbed in the mid-eighties, so I sold it for more than what we paid. I can only imagine what it would sell for now. An architectural gem, Marvin called it. He knew more about that kind of thing than I did. But it was solid, two fireplaces, hardwood floors, nice layout, and a great backyard. Everything we dreamed of; close to the club where Marvin performed, and a short bus ride from my work. Lots of stairs, though, which became a problem. Paying for it became a problem too, and then after Marvin passed..."

"What year did he die?" Bruce asked.

"Technically in 1982, but the man I loved died on May 21, 1979, the night of the White Night Riots." Hank slid into the passenger seat, thoughts of that May night percolating in his head. "Have I ever told you about the day I met Jerry Garcia?" he asked with exaggerated enthusiasm, hoping to redirect the conversation.

What followed was a short back-and-forth treatise on the songs and career trajectory of the Grateful Dead before Bruce pulled out onto the street.

"Listen, I was thinking I'd swing by my sister's place while we're on the west side," Bruce said. "She's got a double-bed mattress she wants to get rid of. Could you use such a thing?"

"God love you, man. I scrounged some pallets and covered them with sheets of Styrofoam I found in the dumpster by Shoppers, but it's still a hard bed. How much does she want for it?"

"Not a cent," Bruce replied. "It would probably go to the curb if you didn't take it, so you're doing her a favour."

Hank swallowed any embarrassment or false pride that might cause him to refuse a free mattress that would be a whole lot more comfortable than what he'd been sleeping on lately. "Okay then, if that's your line, I'd be happy to help her out. God, it will be like sleeping at the Delta!"

1983

Hank pulled up the flap and took the brown envelope out of the mailbox. He recognized his mother's handwriting and felt the familiar tug of guilt and regret her correspondence always elicited. She always jotted a few sentences down on whatever paper accompanied the photographs she sent. Those had come quite regularly, and as much as he loved seeing Jennifer's growth from grade to grade, it always served to remind him what a shithead father he was.

Marvin had always made sure each photograph was framed and displayed prominently in the house, often referring to the little girl as their daughter.

"She'd be lucky to have two such great dads," friends would say.

Jennifer's graduation picture had been the last one Marvin framed.

Several photographs spilled out onto the kitchen table. Sorting through them, it took Hank a few seconds to realize the baby boy was his grandson. A few of the photos had a beaming Jennifer holding her infant son. *Ryan Franklin Davis 6lb 3oz, born February 3rd, 1983* was printed on the back of one.

Hank sat down and lowered his head into his hands as the sobbing began.

"He'd be a lucky little boy to have two such great granddads." That could not be said now, Hank thought, even if he ever got the privilege of meeting his grandson. But maybe with Marvin gone it was time to go back home.

1983

Jenny Davis pulled the mesh over the top of the open carriage. Thumping the wheels down the steep back stairs while juggling a screaming baby had drawn the attention of everyone on the street, but no one had offered to help or even bothered to say hello. Trevor had thought it was such a good idea to move to Hampton, but he wasn't the one alone here all day with a colicky baby. And so far, this small, "friendly" town did not feel the least bit friendly.

"This is a perfect place to raise a family and it's far enough away from both our families that they won't always be in our business."

Jenny wasn't sure why it annoyed Trevor so much that his parents cared about him enough to check in every day. His family and how involved they were had drawn her to Trevor Davis in the first place. Jenny loved Trevor's mother, and from the beginning had often imagined Frank was her own father.

"Ryan Franklin," the nurse repeated while filling out the information for the baby's birth certificate. "Is Franklin your father's name?"

As her sweet boy latched onto her breast, the flinch of pain mirrored the internal jolt she always felt when asked about her father. Everyone assumed Terry was her father, but she'd always cleared that mistake up right away. Still, she never followed up her vehement denial of Terry with any information about her real father. She knew very little about him, anyway; Mom had never seen fit to share any details, and it seemed easier to let on he was dead.

Henry Vincent Lowman. A name on a wrinkled, faded birth certificate.

"Yes, Franklin is my father's name," Jenny answered.

December 7, 2021

*P*earl pulled out a package of licorice from her shopping bag, ripped out a piece, and passed it to Hank. "Quite the storm last night, eh?"

"Yeah. It was a wild one."

"Where did you sleep, if you don't mind my asking?"

Hank shuffled a bit, kicking at a piece of garbage on the ground in front of the bench. He woke at sunrise surprised he'd slept, relieved that everything still seemed to be intact. He had covered the mattress securely with garbage bags to keep out the dampness, so it was still good. Some rain had seeped in under the tarp, soaking some clothes. He'd dumped the sodden pile into a dumpster, as he had no hope of drying them.

"I have a place off of Carleton."

"A place? With a roof, Hank?"

"Kind of."

"No shame in it, you know."

"Really?" Hank looked around at the few people outside. He'd been surprised to see Pearl walk up and sit down a few minutes ago; the wind was bitter and everything still damp and cold. Not a morning for hanging out in King's Square.

"I was walking back from Shoppers and I saw you leaving your place," Pearl said. "Must have been a nasty night for you."

"Truth be told, Pearl, my present accommodation isn't the worst I've had. One of the boarding houses I lived in had a stench I can't even describe. And the rodents who occupied that space were probably the friendliest of the creatures who lived there. At least I live alone where I am now."

"I live alone too," Pearl replied. "I'm going to take my shopping home. I'll bring you back a coffee. Are you going to be here for a while?"

"Don't have anywhere else to be."

Pearl picked up her bags and headed across the square. She had almost suggested Hank come home with her to get out of the cold for a while. The words had been on the tip of her tongue, but debilitating panic and fear had choked them back down. At the crosswalk she turned her head to make sure no cars were coming, pulled up her hood, and picked up her pace.

1983

Mary left school between English and Biology and started walking toward Bayside Drive. She'd walked almost to the refinery before someone finally stopped to pick her up. Jane had offered to go with her, saying she shouldn't hitchhike alone. She told Jane she'd be fine. Her drive let her out before the causeway, and Mary headed up the hill toward Dr. Winter's office. With the wind full in the face, her eyes blurred with tears. Her father's words echoed in her head: "You're a little tramp, just like your mother. You'll get yourself knocked up and tie some poor bugger to you and your bastard kid. That apple didn't fall too far from the tree."

She was determined to prove her father wrong. It was common knowledge that Dr. Winters gave out birth control, no questions asked. Nothing had happened yet between her and Gary, but she wasn't taking any chances. The last thing Mary MacAllister needed was to get saddled with a kid at fifteen. She wasn't going to follow in her mother's footsteps and end up raising kids in a shithole apartment in the south end of Saint John.

December 7, 2021

Miriam laid the paintings out on her kitchen table. She'd selected a couple to give as gifts to clients but had decided soon after ordering them that she'd keep most of them for herself. Her small apartment was already ridiculously decorated with a nautical theme as if it were a quaint seaside cottage. Or a bungalow on the Kennebecasis River.

She'd gone way overboard with the theme, but she owed no one an explanation. She seldom had company in this small apartment, but she proudly claimed to live in the valley. For a brief time, she'd come close to having a Kennebecasis Park address, but her short relationship with the guy who owned that house had fizzled almost as quickly as her marriage had a few years before.

Miriam looked around the room at the mishmash of furnishings and decor. The realtor in her bristled at the display. If she had hired someone to stage this room, she'd not be using their services again. Maybe Gloria Hamilton's artwork would perk the room up.

1984

"You don't have to clean every time you visit, Jenny, dear. Your grand-father and I do fine, and we have a woman coming in one day a week. We just love getting a chance to see that little boy."

"I don't mind at all, Nan. I'll just finish vacuuming and then I'll get us some lunch. I brought you a pot of turkey soup. We can have some, and there'll still be plenty left for a few meals for you and Grampie."

Ryan zoomed his toy truck in and out of the legs of the chair that Doris Bennett was sitting on. Gordon was sound asleep on the couch across the room, seemingly oblivious to the noise of a toddler and the whir of the Electrolux.

A few minutes later Jenny lifted Ryan into the highchair. She dished up two bowls of soup and set them down in front of her grandparents.

"You are too good to us," Nan said.

"Do you want some crackers, Grampie?" Jenny asked.

Gordon nodded and Jenny went to the cupboard.

"Don't know what we'd do without you and your mother," Grampie said. "Couldn't ask for a better daughter or granddaughter, and now this darling little boy too."

Doris spooned some soup into Ryan's mouth. His gurgling lips sent the liquid spraying out. She laughed as she wiped his little cheeks with her napkin.

"What a precious gift this little boy is," Nan said. "Babies bring such joy to a family."

Gordon broke crackers into his bowl of soup and chuckled. "I recall you having a much different outlook on that when our daughter told us she was pregnant. Seems to me you hid in the house for months."

"Now, why would you say such a thing?" Nan grumbled.

"Well, that's the truth, woman. You were so concerned about what the church folks would think, and then when her marriage ended you stopped going out altogether."

"Ridiculous what I put myself through, thinking God was punishing me. The church had me brainwashed, but somewhere along the way I started waking up. I stopped being so scared of what everyone else thought."

As Gordon Bennett spooned up the last of his soup, he started coughing, his body rocking and his face becoming beet red. Jenny stopped what she was doing and went to his side.

"Are you all right, Grampie? That cough sounds terrible."

"I've been telling him that," Nan said. "The stubborn old fool won't go to the doctor."

"I'm fine," Gordon said. "What's the doctor going to do?"

Jenny poured tea for her grandparents and sat to finish feeding Ryan.

"God gave me a beautiful granddaughter," Nan said. "Once I held you in my arms, I wouldn't have changed anything. I knew the day I met your father that he was only marrying your mother because he thought that's what he should do, but it wasn't until later that I realized what I picked up on that day. Your father wasn't the first man to marry a woman to escape the condemnation they knew family and society would dish out."

"What do you mean, Nan?" Jenny asked.

"I don't suppose your mother ever told you, but she figured out early on in their marriage that Hank was hiding something. But maybe you should ask her what she thinks the main reason was your father couldn't stay. Things were really hard for men like him in this city back then."

"Are you saying my father is gay?" Jenny asked.

"Yes, although that's not the word we used to use. Back then 'gay' meant 'happy.'"

"So, you think my father left because he was gay?"

"I don't know, dear. But one thing I am sure about is that whatever his reason for leaving Tanya and Saint John, he adored you."

"He did?"

"Yes, he did. He was a good father, Jenny, and I'm ashamed I never told you that."

"Mom's never told me anything about him."

"She had to move on and make a new life for herself. You were so young when your father left, and I'm sure she wanted you to think of Terry as a father. We should have told you more. No matter what, Hank was still your dad, and you deserved to know about him."

Jenny lifted Ryan out of the highchair before slumping into the rocking chair, overwhelmed with the information Nan had just delivered. Her nausea and panic had nothing to do with learning her father was gay. How she was feeling was coming from the slow release of the anger and resentment she'd used her whole life to shield herself from longing for the father she barely knew. The father she obviously knew nothing about. Why was it then, that she could still remember what it felt like to be swooped up into his arms?

"I better change this little guy, Nan," Jenny said. "I think I smell poop."

December 7, 2021

*P*earl sat down on the bench beside Hank. From a large blue-and-white-striped bag, she pulled out a thermos, two coffee mugs, and a bag of Mrs. Dunster's doughnuts. "We'll have a feast. The wind's died down a bit and the sky looks brighter."

"Thanks a lot, Pearl. I appreciate this little picnic. Nothing like hands around a hot mug of coffee. Paper cups just aren't the same."

Pearl poured coffee into the two big mugs and handed one to Hank. She took a swig from hers before speaking. "I need to tell you something, Hank."

"What, did you win the lottery or something?"

"No, I didn't win the lottery, but wouldn't that be something if I did. First thing I'd do is buy a big fancy place we could both live in. It's about that. I feel guilty every time I leave you and walk to my apartment."

"What do you mean?" Hank said, reaching for a doughnut. "What do you have to feel guilty about?"

"I have a roof over my head, running hot and cold water, heat, a stove to cook on, and a refrigerator to keep food in. I have all the comforts of home—nothing fancy, but a safe and comfortable place to lay my head every night."

"And I'm glad you do," Hank said, turning toward Pearl. "I don't begrudge anyone that can say the same. I hope I don't act like I do."

"No, that's the thing, you never seem angry about how unfair it is that someone like me has a place I can afford to live in and you don't. But I feel angry at myself. I have a comfortable couch, and if I was any kind of friend, I'd invite you to sleep on it, especially with winter coming on."

"Pearl, don't be ridiculous. You certainly don't need to feel guilty for my present housing situation."

"I want to tell you why I can't offer you a place to stay until your situation gets better."

"You do not owe me an explanation," Hank said firmly. "You don't owe me anything."

Pearl poured more coffee into both cups before continuing. "I have not had an easy life, Hank. I made some bad choices and I burned a lot of bridges. But some of what happened to me was not my fault. I've had some very bad men in my life."

"I'm sorry to hear that, Pearl."

"My father used to beat me. He beat us all. You'd think that would teach a girl to stay away from violent men, but I married one every bit as angry and cruel as my father. I had kids with him, even when I knew he'd be as terrible a father as my own. I just drank myself into a daze and ignored it. My escape from him came when he died in a barroom brawl, but I didn't get myself straightened out. Instead, I fell for a charmer I met in Queen Square and believed every word the silver-tongued devil told me. Just weeks after meeting him I invited him to move in, and the terror he inflicted made my dad and my husband seem like saints."

Pearl pulled a Kleenex out of her coat pocket and dabbed her eyes before continuing.

"I don't trust anybody. I got myself sober, but I carry a lot of baggage. My own kids don't even talk to me, and I have never met my grandchildren. I am a lonely, scared old woman, and my little apartment with its deadbolt locks is the only place I feel safe."

Hank shifted his mug to his other hand and draped his free arm around Pearl's shoulder. "I am so sorry to hear you've been through all that, Pearl. Believe me, I know what it's like to feel unsafe and afraid. The violence I've been afraid of comes from hatred and intolerance. I'm an old man now, and I don't give off any gay vibes, but believe me, I know what terror can come from just walking down the street. And sometimes violence bursts right through doors, finds and attacks victims just for being a certain way and in a certain place." He set his coffee cup down on the ground and reached to embrace Pearl in a hug. "You have every right to take care of yourself first, and I'm glad you feel safe in your apartment. I think you're a courageous, amazing woman."

Pearl returned the hug awkwardly, then repositioned herself on the bench. "I just didn't want you to think I don't care."

"I never thought that for one minute, Pearl. Would someone who didn't care make such good coffee and bring a man a whole bag of doughnuts? I'll take another one of those."

1985

Hank stood inside the front door, looking down the hall toward the living room and bedrooms and into the large, sunny kitchen. This had been such a lovely home, and leaving it was so difficult, but no more difficult than the last few years had been. Somehow, he'd pulled himself up from the darkness he'd plunged into after Marvin's funeral. He'd gone back to work after two weeks in the psych ward and carried on as best he could, even as the scourge of AIDS took friends and others succumbed to the attacks on and following the night of the brutal attack on Marvin. Where was the hope Harvey Milk had dreamed of?

This golden city held nothing more for him, and signing the sales agreement this morning had made that even clearer than giving his notice at Western last week. The recording business was in as much change and uncertainty as life in Castro these days.

Hank wasn't even sure when thoughts of going back home had surfaced. It started with some dreams that randomly took him to places like Gran's kitchen, Tin Can Beach, Dykeman's hardware store, and the ball field at Tucker Park. Who was even left in Saint John that he cared about? Besides Jennifer, of course, and his grandson, who would now be two years old.

Making the decision to return to Saint John brought no joy but somehow a sense of relief. Being in this house and walking down the streets he and Marvin had walked together was excruciating. Every detail only reminded him of his loss. *Sorry for your loss* had been the repeated mantra as he stumbled through the days after Marvin died. Each time those words were offered, Hank had bristled and pushed down his rage.

A blessing, some said. *He's in a better place,* a particularly offensive line. The real sorrow and tragedy of all of this was the hatred, intolerance, and revenge that had provoked police officers to storm the club and drag

Marvin from his dressing room. Had anything changed in the years following? Small, hopeful steps, like a high school bearing Harvey Milk's name opening in April in the East Village of New York, were just grains of sand. And Dan White's suicide in October hadn't put an end to the tsunami of suffering his bullets had provoked.

::

Jenny and her mother walked up the steps of Brenan's Funeral Home. Two funerals within four months of each other, this one even smaller than the last. Her grandparents' siblings and most of their friends were already dead, so it made for a small crowd gathering for final goodbyes to Annette Lowman in Brenan's chapel this afternoon.

Before taking her seat, Jenny walked over to the picture board and quickly scanned it, looking for pictures of her father. There were several of him when he was a little boy, and a couple of him as a teenager around the time he would have met her mother. The man in the photograph looked nothing like Glen Campbell. Jenny pulled one the snapshots from the board and slipped it into her purse.

December 7, 2021

Hank walked down the street, glad to have the strong wind pushing him along instead of hitting him in the face. The thermos of hot coffee Pearl had brought had only done so much to combat the damp chill penetrating the layers of his clothing. Walking would help warm him. Maybe he'd stop in and visit Gloria for a bit. He remembered as a kid running to his grandmother's house, excited to enter the warmth provided by her coal-fired stove. She always welcomed him with tight hugs and home-baked goodies. Here he was, now several years older than she'd been then, and still in need of comfort and a place to belong.

Gloria saw Hank on the sidewalk before he stepped up to ring the bell. She'd woken in the night worried about where he might be as the rain hit the tin roof and the wind rocked her two-storey farmhouse. He'd still been on her mind as she drove into the city, and she had scanned the uptown streets, hoping to catch a glimpse of him.

"You must be frozen," Gloria said as she opened the door and motioned for Hank to come in.

"A bit damp and chilled. Not the nicest day."

"I've got the space heater going in the studio. Take your wet coat off and sit in front of it. I brought you in a couple of pairs of Ted's heavy socks if you want to put on a pair now. Are your feet wet? What about your pants? Are they wet?"

Hank removed his parka and hung it on an empty hook. He slipped off his boots and pulled up his thin socks.

"My grannie used to keep socks and mittens on a line in her kitchen. We'd come in and strip our icy ones off and put the toasty warm ones on. I'll take the socks, but my pants are fine. Can't have Ted finding out some strange man steps in your door and the first thing he does is take his pants off."

Hank walked into the studio. The heat and comfort of the small space hit him immediately.

"I've told Ted all about you. He knows you're a friend and nothing for him to worry about."

"Because I'm gay?" Hank chuckled.

"No," Gloria replied. "Because you're a good guy."

Hank sat down on the couch, slipped off his socks, and rubbed his numb toes before quickly pulling on the new socks. The glimpse of his disgusting toenails and discoloured feet brought a lump to his throat. This generous woman did not need to see that.

"I could take those socks home and wash them for you," Gloria said.

"Don't bother. Best thing would be to pitch them." Hank scooped the socks up off the floor and quickly deposited them in the garbage can in the front hall. Coming back in the room, he stood close to the space heater, hoping his pants would dry quickly and not give off much of a stench. "I'm an old man still letting women look after me as if I was a helpless kid. Two of my best friends right now are women older than my grandmother was when I was a boy. I thought she was ancient, but now I realize she was twenty years younger than I am right now."

"I suppose I should be insulted that you're calling me old, but calling me a best friend makes up for that. That's what I told Ted yesterday. You are a good friend already, after just a couple of weeks. I don't think he got it at first."

"You have no idea how much I look forward to walking along Germain and coming to your door," Hank said. "Seeing your light on helps get me through these dreary days."

"I wish I could do more. Giving you a bowl of soup now and then and offering you new socks doesn't seem like enough."

Hank turned toward Gloria. "I'm not your responsibility. God, you do more than the hundreds of people that pass me on the street in the run of a day. They pretend I'm not there and tell themselves all the others like me are just as unimportant."

Gloria set a blank canvas on the easel.

"I should be doing more for all of those people. I drive or walk by them too and tell myself a yearly donation to the United Way or taking a box of food to Romero House occasionally is doing enough."

"I don't have the answer for that, Gloria. I just know that from the first day we met you've treated me with nothing but kindness and respect. But just like any new friendship, there is a lot we can learn about each other. Some days I want to unload it all on you, tell you every sad detail and every shitty thing that got me here. But I want to tell you the good things too, because there were so many of those."

Gloria walked to the sink and filled her water jar. Emotion surfaced as a silence hung in the room. "I hope you will do that, and let me do the same," she finally said. "I know I dwell too much on my loss sometimes, but I've had lots of joy in my life too. And lots of blessings. But I feel guilty going home to my warm house not knowing where you are sleeping and where you'll get your next meal."

"You're the second woman to tell me that today. But like I told her, you're not to blame. Your blessings are deserved, you worked hard for the comforts you have, and you have nothing to apologize for. Friends don't have to have the same circumstances and live the same kind of lives. Friends just need to care, and you have already done plenty of caring."

Before sitting down again Hank unzipped the leather pouch around his waist and removed his Tin Can Beach postcard.

"Every time I pull this postcard out, your friendship is right there with me. In your own way you make everything better without swooping in and taking all the shitty parts away."

"But would it be so bad if I did?" Gloria asked. "What if I could convince Ted to let you move in with us? We have the great big house we raised four kids in, now with three empty bedrooms. Would it be so bad to just let you have a warm bedroom and the guarantee of three good meals a day?"

"I don't want you beating yourself up like that, Gloria. I wish it was that easy and every empty bedroom in the country could house a homeless person. But the problem is more complicated than that."

"It seems to me it's just that simple," Gloria said, her voice rising with emotion. "But Ted would say I was naive."

"You're just a nice person, and the world needs more of those. Listen, if I'm keeping you from painting this morning, just tell me. I'm warmer and these heavy socks are great. My parka has probably dried some."

Gloria set the water jar down on her work table before pulling up a chair close to Hank. "Tell me one of your blessings."

"Marvin," Hank said. "Marvin was the second man I loved, the one I thought I'd live out my life with. But that brings up a bad thing, and I will stay on the good. Marvin was beautiful. Honestly, when he dressed himself up, at first glance you'd think him the most stunning woman you'd ever laid eyes on. Maybe today he would be someone who might consider transitioning. Who knows? But Marvin was perfectly confident and happy in exactly who he was, and he was the man who made me finally accept who I was. Now your turn."

"I was a terrible student and frittered away my high school years," Gloria began.

"I thought you were telling me a good thing."

"I am," Gloria said. "I always wanted to be a teacher, but I convinced myself I was stupid. I was lazy, but I wasn't stupid. I took the easy path in school and was a major underachiever. I graduated and got a job in a jewellery store, but I still wanted to be a teacher. To make a long story short, I finally got off my ass and did something about it. I went to university as a mature student on a probationary basis and found out I wasn't one bit stupid. I finished a four-year degree in three years. I got married and had Zachary. When he was nine months old, I went back to university and got my education degree and I got a job teaching the next year. I taught elementary school for thirty years and loved it."

"See, I told you, you worked for what you have," Hank said.

"What work did you love, Hank?"

"I will tell you about that someday. It was one of the things that made me leave Saint John in the first place."

Gloria got up, realizing the time. "I'll make us some lunch."

"Can I help you?" Hank asked, following Gloria out to the kitchen.

"You can butter the rolls. I'm just going to heat up this soup."

Hank pulled two rolls out of the bag and began buttering them. "Do you think it's all right to line up the accomplishments you've had beside the things you've messed up, your failures?" he asked. "Or is doing that just a way to make ourselves feel less guilty?"

Gloria stirred the soup, thinking about Hank's question. "It's the yin and the yang. The joys and the sorrow, the dark and the light. It's just…life."

1986

The bus ride home was so different from the one Hank took to leave. Instead of the stops and several months of working along the way, Hank made the trip from California to Calais, Maine, in five days. Several times on the journey he found himself wondering why he had decided to return to Saint John. He had held on as long as he could, but San Francisco offered only sad reminders of the life he and Marvin had built together. Saint John didn't have much to offer, but somehow Hank felt drawn back there.

He arrived in Saint John after midnight and walked from the bus station to the Holiday Inn on Haymarket Square. He took the cheapest room available and slept well into the afternoon the next day. Walking outside, he breathed in the damp air and felt the fog envelop him. All his senses screamed *Saint John* and a panic rose in his chest. What the hell had he been thinking?

Hank walked quickly to Reggie's Restaurant and devoured the daily special. Looking around, he took in the familiar surroundings and thought back to the many times he'd sat here with George. Hot turkey sandwich, extra peas, and a side heap of french fries slathered in gravy had always been George's order. It was always entertaining to watch George savour the meal and flirt with the waitress.

Hank slid the last morsel onto his fork, thinking of what a performance it all had been. As a teenager he'd been careful to dress and act the part of a red-blooded male with nothing but girls and getting laid on his mind. George did the same, and to see them no one would have guessed the inner turmoil they both felt. It would have been unthinkable to drop the façade.

Hank had been a master of hiding it even from himself, and his relationship with Tanya had been part of that deception. Her getting pregnant

SUSAN WHITE

seemed at the time almost a gift that would protect him and mask his true inclinations. When he did finally leave, he'd fooled himself into believing it was only to follow his dream of producing music and nothing else motivating his escape.

So here he was back in his hometown, the place he'd spent his early life pretending to be someone he wasn't. He had no intention of hiding who he was, but knew being vocal about it was still not a smart thing to do, even in 1986.

Marvin always took that "loud and proud" approach, and look what had happened to him. Hank wasn't afraid to die but was not going to invite every narrow-minded homophobe to beat the gay out of him either. It didn't matter anymore anyway. He would blend in, hide away in this familiar city, and go through the motions of living. Nothing else mattered to him.

"Any work at the port these days?" Hank asked the man sitting in the booth across from him.

"Saint John's a big shithole right now. Elsie goes on and on about it being the greatest little city in the east, but it's shutdown after shutdown. Some French company bought the sugar refinery and God knows when they'll shut that down. Tearing down Union Station was the first nail in this city's coffin. Shipping and the railway are the lifeblood of this city. You tell me how some old broad from the floodplains of Glen Falls would know anything about running a city."

"Any thoughts where I could get work?"

"Try the oil refinery or the pulp mill. It's an Irving town now, boy."

Hank walked to the counter to pay his bill. It was just a short walk to the Golden Ball. He'd go there and ask if they were hiring. And once he got settled, found work and a place to live, he would try to contact Jennifer and maybe even get to meet his grandson.

December 8, 2021

Jen looked at the clock and was surprised by how much time she'd spent scrolling, listening to recordings of songs, and watching YouTube biographies. When she sat down to do her banking she hadn't planned on wasting the next hour on a Google search of Glen Campbell. But this morning she'd woken up from a dream that held the echo of the familiar introduction: "Good evening, ladies and gentlemen, I'm Glen Campbell."

Her ten-year-old brain had fabricated a fantasy that she held tightly for the three years of Glen Campbell's weekly show. Each time a Glen Campbell song played on the radio the fantasy would swell and she would elaborate on the scenario of the day he'd arrive to take her to his California mansion. But by the time "Rhinestone Cowboy" came out, she was sixteen and had given that fantasy up. She replaced it with anger, resentment, and the belief she'd not been reason enough for her father to stick around.

Had she ever spoken the words of her imagined paternity to anyone before she'd confessed it to Miriam? Thoughts of Glen Campbell were so mixed up with the longing she'd felt lately to find her father. Did it have to do with the fact she would soon have to say a final goodbye to her mother?

How could she mourn losing a father she'd never known? A blurry picture of him as a teenager was all she had. And his full name on her birth certificate, as if that gave her anything at all.

Jen clicked to continue watching the video. Alcohol and cocaine use, three divorces. Through blurry eyes she focused on the gaunt and desperate man on the screen looking nothing like the man she'd held in such high regard. Glen Campbell had eight children and had been absent most of the time with the first five. After his death three children were reportedly left out of the will. This man she'd put high on a pedestal and imagined to be the perfect father was far from that. He had been human and made bad choices and terrible mistakes.

Jen pulled a Kleenex from the box and let her tears come. She felt compassion and sadness for the old man on the screen, frail and struggling with disease. This man who had been dead for four years still held such a place in her heart, simply because she had pretended as a kid that he was her missing father. Surely to God she could find a measure of compassion to forgive the man who really had fathered her, even if he'd been absent her whole life.

Was he still alive? Did he still live in California? She wished she'd asked her mother and grandparents more about him. All her grandparents were gone, and her mother was mostly incoherent with the drug regimen keeping her pain at bay.

1987

ank pushed his cleaning cart through the elevator door. Being the night janitor at the Golden Ball lacked the creative fulfillment and monetary rewards of his last job, but there was something about moving through this empty building at night that suited him right now. After finishing his shift, he always walked home on the dark, empty streets, and drank a pint of vodka before finally falling asleep in his small room in the Princess Street boarding house. He had his one meal a day at Reggie's then took a quick walk-about in King's Square, always ending up on a bench directly across from the refurbished Imperial Theatre. He'd sit there a while before heading down the street to start his shift. Monday to Friday provided him a predicable routine. It was the weekends that were proving the most difficult and the loneliest.

Elevator music was an abomination, and Hank always bristled at the generic tunes that played as he made his way to the top floor. Tonight's instrumental rendering of "California Dreamin" was especially disconcerting. Hank welled up with the memory of his first studio session, recording this song. He'd been on top of the world looking through the glass as the four singers delivered their vocals. The cutting-edge, important work, the realization of his long-held dream, had made him feel more alive than he'd ever felt.

The way he felt now as his nightly drunken state gave him some reprieve from the misery he carried every day was a dark contrast. Maybe coming back to Saint John was a self-flagellating act, punishment for not being able to keep Marvin alive.

The elevator doors opened and Hank stepped away from the music. Having no music in his life was another way he was paying penance. The few seconds of elevator tunes he heard every night certainly did not count.

SUSAN WHITE

December 10, 2021

Jenny kept pacing, keeping her eye on the arrivals board. If she sat down, she'd probably fall asleep. Last night she'd hardly slept stretched out on the couch in the family room in the palliative care unit after the nurse had convinced her to leave her mother's bedside.

"She is not likely to pass tonight, Jen. I will keep checking, and if I see any change, I will wake you."

Ryan's flight was delayed. Luckily, she'd seen that when she checked his flight status earlier and hadn't rushed to meet his eleven o'clock flight. She had hoped Trevor would offer to pick Ryan up so that she wouldn't have to leave the hospital. He knew she'd been keeping a round-the-clock vigil at her mother's bedside. Ryan was his son too, for goodness' sake, but she guessed his new wife and new family were more important than the one he'd discarded ten years ago.

"The twins are teething and we've been up with them most nights, Jen. I'll call Ryan tomorrow and set something up."

Trevor had had several relationships after their marriage ended and finally married a woman twenty years younger than himself and started a second family right away. It seemed he was much more involved with raising them than he'd ever been in raising Ryan.

"You could just bring them along to the airport if they aren't sleeping anyway. Ryan would love to see his sisters."

"Don't be so ridiculous."

Ten years ago, she had been ridiculous, thinking their distance and unhappiness were nothing more than a midlife crisis. It had taken her months to realize Trevor's frequent absences were because of an affair with a coworker. It had also been ridiculous just how much she didn't care when he finally came clean. She guessed early rejection from the first man in your life prepares you for a cheating husband. It had been a relief when he moved out. It hadn't been easy for Ryan, though.

Arrived came on the screen and Jenny walked to the big window to watch the airplane turn and come to a stop. This visit was not going to be a happy one, but hopefully Ryan would get to see his grandmother alive and say his goodbyes. They would get a good night's sleep first and go to the hospital in the morning.

1988

ank walked the length of Edith Street twice before deciding which house was the Bennetts'. God, he'd lived here for a few months before he and Tanya moved into the flat on Lansdowne, but very little about this house looked as he remembered it. Finally, it was the oddly shaped front porch that convinced him. Walking up the path, he wondered what he'd say and what reception he'd get if either of Tanya's parents answered the door.

Hank recalled the first day he'd met the Bennetts. After the long, uncomfortable church service, he'd squeezed into the back seat of their Oldsmobile beside Tanya. The short drive across the causeway seemed torturous, knowing the bombshell she planned on dropping after dinner. But somehow, he'd managed to eat the roast beef dinner and a good-sized piece of lemon pie. Hank hadn't been fond of lemon pie since.

A noticeably pregnant young woman opened the door a crack.

"Do the Bennetts live here?" Hank asked.

"No," the woman answered.

"This was their house in 1959, I believe," Hank said, knowing how dumb that sounded. "Any idea where they live now?"

"No, I don't. We bought this house two years ago. I'm not sure what the people's names were who sold it. Marjorie might know." The woman pointed to the house next door. "She's lived here forever."

"Thank you. Sorry to bother you."

Hank walked back out to the sidewalk and turned toward the yellow house where the woman indicated Marjorie lived. He could see an older woman sitting on the stoop.

"Did I hear you asking about the Bennetts?" the woman hollered. "Not a politician, are ya? That's all we have knocking on our doors these days it seems. They all want to stick their signs on my lawn. I tell them where they can stick their signs."

"Are you Marjorie?" Hank asked.

"Yes, who's asking? An old lady can't be giving too much information out these days."

"The woman next door said you might know the Bennetts."

Marjorie stood up and hobbled toward Hank. "Do you want to tell me who you are first? Not a bill collector, are ya?"

"I was married to the Bennetts' daughter Tanya."

"You that fella that up and left her with that precious little girl?"

Hank followed the woman back to her yard. "Yeah, that's me. Guilty as charged. Do you know where the Bennetts are living now?"

"Only one still living, and poor Doris might as well be gone. She's not known anyone for a spell. She's at the Villa. Last I checked, anyway. I've not seen her in the obits, so I reckon she's still there. I don't find it as easy to get around these days and haven't gotten over to visit her in some time. Seemed kind of pointless the last time anyway. Gordon died around two years ago, I'd say. He had the lung cancer. He was really bad at the last of it, but Doris looked after him right to the end. I figure that's what made her go wonky."

"You wouldn't know where Tanya lives, or my daughter, Jennifer? I've got a grandson too, about five now I think."

A few minutes later Hank walked away knowing a bit more than when he arrived. Marjorie said Tanya had remarried some guy Terry and lived somewhere on the way to Moncton. She only knew that because Doris used to say at least they didn't have to go all the way to Moncton every time they visited. Marjorie also told him Jennifer had bought a house in Hampton. Doris and Gordon had helped her with the down payment.

December 13, 2021

*G*loria stepped out on her stoop and scanned the sidewalk up and down and across the street. At suppertime last night she had again brought up the subject of extending an invitation to Hank to live with them for the winter at least.

"He's eighty-one years old, Ted. Surely you see how sad that is."

Ted stacked the plates and made his way to the dishwasher. "Yes, it is very sad, but we can't just open our house up to all the sad cases."

"Imagine if your dad had had to live on the street or in a makeshift shelter when he was that age. Wouldn't you have wanted someone to extend some compassion?"

"Well, of course I would. But my father worked hard all his life and had a house, savings, and a pension to see him through. How come this guy doesn't?"

"He had a job, owned a house in California, had a partner and a life. He's had some hard knocks. Maybe he even made what you might call bad choices, but a lot was out of his control. I would think you could understand that. And what about 'There, but for the grace of God, go I'? Life doesn't work out for everyone, you know. I don't see why we can't share some of our good fortune."

Ted had shut the discussion down using the excuse of going to put wood in the furnace.

Gloria saw Miriam Ross approaching.

"Good morning, Gloria," Miriam called out. "A bit chilly to be out in your shirt sleeves."

Gloria remembered the judgement she'd heard in this woman's words the last time and didn't offer an explanation.

"Not giving art lessons to that old guy this morning?"

"His name is Hank," Gloria replied, even though Miriam didn't seem interested and had breezed into the studio ahead of her.

1988

Hank dropped the money into the slot of the pay phone and carefully dialled the number. A long shot, but finding out Jennifer's married name was the first thing he needed to do. Getting an address and finding a way to Hampton would be the next.

"Loch Lomond Villa," said a sugary sweet voice.

Hank cleared his throat before beginning his rehearsed dialogue. "Good morning. I was supposed to meet my daughter there this morning but something came up and I'm running late. I wouldn't want her to worry. I was hoping you could give her a message for me. Can you check to see if she's there yet? Do you have a visitor's log or something?"

"What is your daughter's name, and who would she be visiting?"

"She'd be visiting Doris Bennett. Her name is Jennifer Lowman."

"I see a Jennifer Davis listed as a contact for Mrs. Bennett. Would that be her?"

Hank hung up. He'd gotten what he was after, and giving Jennifer a message from a father she never had was not necessary. Something came up all right, and he was definitely running late. About twenty-eight years too late.

Hank pulled the telephone book off the shelf underneath the pay-phone. He leafed through to find the Hampton section. Davis. There were five listed, four of which had addresses beside the name. He ripped the page from the book, folded it, and put it in his shirt pocket. He slipped the book back onto the shelf and left the booth.

December 13, 2021

Miriam set the bags down on the seat beside her then reached into her purse for her cellphone. Before driving to her next appointment, she would send Jenny a quick text. It was probably a long shot, but Gloria had said the homeless guy's name was Hank. His age fit, and Hank wasn't an overly common name. She'd tell Jenny even though she knew how busy these days were for her. Ryan had been home for the weekend, and of course she was still going to the hospital every day. Probably the last bit of news she needed was the possibility that her father was a down-and-out old man living on the street.

Gloria hadn't actually said the man was homeless. Maybe Miriam was jumping to conclusions based on the way he was dressed and his smell. Some might say she was a bit of a snob and quick to categorize people. There might be a grain of truth to that, but not having a Pollyanna approach to life, she called it as she saw it. And growing up in the south end, she'd seen her share of bums and vagrants.

In fact, her father often entertained the down-and-outers, not the least bit concerned that there were young girls in the house. Miriam had had to get resourceful more than once when the party got out of hand. At least this Hank guy didn't smell of alcohol. She knew that smell only too well, and her aversion to it had kept her from going down the same road as her father.

Unfortunately, it hadn't kept her from marrying an alcoholic, though at least she'd realized it quickly. "Fuck this shit," she'd said and walked out after two years, determined to make a life she could be proud of. She had worked so hard to establish a professional persona and reputation that helped erase the shame she felt for being gullible enough to fall in love with Mark Ross.

1988

Hank walked the entire length of Rothesay Avenue, having left Duke at first light. Once on the highway he started thumbing. Walking all the way to Hampton and then trudging from one address to the other, hoping to find the house his daughter lived in, seemed too daunting. Maybe someone would take pity on him and the ride would at least get him to Hampton. Hopefully he would find his daughter today. He'd worry about getting back to the city later. He didn't expect a warm welcome either way, but he had to start somewhere, and finding Jennifer was the first step.

A red half ton slowed and pulled on to the shoulder. Hank ran toward the truck, and after the man gestured for him to get in, he slid into the passenger seat.

"Where you going, buddy?"

"Hampton."

"Well, I'm headed that way. I can drop you off just a bit before the exit. I work at High Low farms. Do you know where that is?"

"No," Hank replied. "I appreciate you stopping, man. Thought I might be here awhile the way cars were zooming by. I don't know the area at all. Grew up in the city but I lived away for more than twenty-five years."

"Where was away?"

"California. San Francisco, mainly."

"Why the hell did you come back here?"

Hank considered his answer, but before speaking the driver spoke again.

"I guess this place ain't so bad. For a city boy I lucked into working at High Low. I love the outdoor work. I'd rather work with a herd of Aberdeen Angus cows than people any day. What'd you do in California?"

"I was a sound engineer in the recording industry back when vinyl was a thing."

"Wow. That sounds exciting. I suppose things changed a lot with the cassette and then the compact disc. This old girl still has an eight-track player, for all the good that is. Can't buy eight tracks any more. The name's Troy, by the way."

"Hank."

"Well, Hank, I get off work at around five o'clock if you're looking for a drive back to the city. You visiting someone?"

"Hope to. Looking to find someone I haven't seen for twenty-nine years. Not sure where exactly they live. We'll see how good my detective skills are."

"Hampton's not that big. Seems like everybody knows everybody there. Ask the first person you see and chances are they'll know where your friend lives."

"My daughter, actually," Hank replied as he got out of the truck.

"Good luck, buddy!"

Hank waved as the guy drove off.

December 14, 2021

Hank woke with a start. Was it the numbing cold or the dream he'd just had? He sat up, grabbing the socks beside his mattress. He stuck his feet out to put them on before getting back into the sleeping bag. He was in no hurry to get up. In this weather he should bed down completely dressed, but he hated staying in the same clothes all the next day.

What had made him dream about the day he'd walked up the street toward the last address on the wrinkled telephone book page? People had answered at the first three addresses, and none of them had been Jennifer. None of them had known her, either, even sharing the same last name. He remembered Troy laughing at that fact on their drive back into Saint John.

"God, I thought everybody in Hampton was related. Went into the Legion with Joe one night and every other guy was his cousin."

No one had been home at the last address. The name on the mailbox beside the front door said *J & T Davis*. A tricycle sat on the front lawn. He'd stood there for a long time, but for some reason could not bring himself to knock on any neighbouring doors to ask who lived in the white bungalow. He felt he had no right to invade and that nobody being home was what he deserved.

Was believing he deserved nothing better what brought him to this sorry state? Was shivering in the bitter cold, hunkered down under a stolen tarp on the side of the causeway, all he deserved? Would things be different if Jennifer had opened the door that day and he had been able to ask her for forgiveness? If he'd been able to watch Ryan sitting on the seat of that red tricycle and maybe been a part of his grandson's life for the last thirty-five years, would everything be different now?

Dreams were cruel and didn't help make these dreadful nights any more bearable. Maybe the only relief he could possibly hope for was that he'd succumb to the cold and his frozen corpse would be found sooner or later.

Hank crawled out of his sleeping bag and pulled on his boots. The lady at Romero House had noticed the state of his old ones and given him this nearly new pair yesterday. Gloria dismissed the value of her donations, but someone had made a huge difference in his life just by dropping these boots off instead of throwing them away or leaving them on the floor of their closet. "The little things matter," Gran had always said, and maybe that little thing would be enough to keep him going one more day.

1990

H ank rolled over, the stream of vomit spraying onto the dirty floor. Why could he not just choke on his own disgusting puke and end his miserable life? At least when he was working, he'd stayed sober all day. But he'd fooled himself into thinking his nighttime drinking didn't matter. Being late most days had been bad enough, but not showing up at all was the straw that broke the camel's back.

"I hate to let you go, Hank. You've been a good worker, but I have no choice. Apparently, the garbage was stinking in the CEO's office when he came in this morning and he told my boss that whoever it was who didn't empty the garbage was to be fired immediately. No point in me trying to plead your case."

What would his case be if Mr. Thorne had pleaded it? It wasn't as if the skills he brought to the job stood for anything. Any idiot could empty garbage cans, vacuum, and wax floors.

Hank recalled his boss at Western going to bat for him after Marvin's attack. The cost of having someone in to care for Marvin quickly became too steep, and he'd asked for reduced hours. Because of his skill and his reputation, they'd let him work a three-day week until even that was not enough. They then let him take a leave of absence so he could give Marvin full-time care. By the time Marvin died, things had changed so much and his heart was no longer in it, so he wasn't long giving his notice. Fortunately, they'd given him a decent severance package and the years he'd spent there provided a small pension.

The knock was faint at first but got louder, making it impossible to ignore even by putting the pillow over his head. Hank got to his feet and went to the door.

"You okay, Hank?"

"Been better."

"Want to go for a coffee?"

Hank focused his blurry eyes on the tall, thin man at his door. His name was Archie, but everyone called him Gramps, as he was by far the oldest man in the rooming house.

"I don't know, Gramps. I'm feeling pretty shitty."

"Fresh air will do you good. My treat. I'll even buy you breakfast if you think you can keep it down."

Hank's head was spinning, and even the thought of food made him nauseous. Last night had been a bad one. He sat to put his sneakers on and followed Gramps out the door. Staying in this stinking room one more minute seemed worse than putting the effort into getting outside.

"I've been there," Gramps said after they'd walked a couple of blocks in silence. "There's only one end to the path you're on."

"Well, if you mean being dead, that's fine with me," Hank said.

"I thought that too. I went as far as trying to speed it up, but God had different plans for me. Put an angel in my path and I'm still here."

"Don't go preaching to me, Gramps. I don't care if you're buying me breakfast, I'm not listening to that shit."

"I get ya. That was the kicker for me when I finally got my sorry arse to a meeting. I'm going to drop it for now, but I am going to keep after you. I've seen too many fellas go down that road. You're entitled to believe what you will, but I believe God let me live and put me where I am to try and help some other poor bugger the way an angel helped me."

December 14, 2021

Jenny parked her car. What the hell was she doing? Was her plan to just walk up and down the streets, maybe through the City Market and into King's Square, looking at every man she saw over seventy who seemed as if he might be living on the street or be down on his luck?

Would she approach any of the men who fit the bill and ask them their names? Or might she just look to see if there was a flicker of recognition either on her part or theirs? Blue eyes, maybe, since blue eyes were the dominant feature they shared.

Miriam had only stated that a man by the name of Hank was hanging around an art studio on Germain. Jenny had gotten her text just as she was leaving the hospital. She was intending to head to the Superstore for a few groceries, run home and unpack them, then maybe have a short nap, but after reading Miriam's text she had driven uptown instead.

Jenny put her gloves on before getting out to pay for parking. How many minutes should she pay for? What was a reasonable amount of time to scout the streets of uptown Saint John looking for a man who might be the father you've not seen in sixty years? How much time to find him, and then how much time would she need if she did?

Jenny put her debit card in the machine and paid for one hour.

The air was chilly, and Jenny hadn't dressed for it. How ridiculous was she to think this was a good idea? Walking down the hill, she slowed in front of a couple of men leaning up against the CIBC on the corner, one of them maybe meeting the criteria she'd established, but the other much younger. They made eye contact and the younger one asked for change. Passing him a loonie, Jenny felt nauseous, not from the interaction but from the fantasy of finding her father being challenged by the stark reality of these two men, no doubt someone else's father, brother, uncle, or son.

Crossing the street, she considered the direction she'd go in next. Maybe she'd walk up through the market and then do a quick walk around King's Square before completely admitting the futility of this walkabout. She heard the ping of a text coming and pulled her phone out of her purse.

A spot has become available at Bobby's Hospice. Your mother will be moved as soon as possible. They are expecting you.

Jenny hurried back to her car. No more hunting for an absent parent when the one she'd always had needed her attention.

1991

H ank had been to three meetings before the mention of Lone Water Farm came up.

"Do I look like a farmer?" Hank asked as he and Gramps left the meeting.

"You don't have to be a farmer. The farm gives you more tools and time away from the mess of the city. You know how hard it is to stay sober here. Surely the great outdoors and a few chores wouldn't kill you."

"Well, how does it work? Can't just show up, can ya?"

"You need a referral from a doctor or a social worker. I could probably get you that."

"Well, shit. Go ahead then. It's not like I have much going on here."

December 14, 2021

"I can't tell you how happy I am that in-person meetings have started up again," Pearl said, sitting down beside Hank on their regular bench. "That Zoom thing is for the birds. I never thought I was a touchy-feely person, but boy I missed those hugs."

"I used to do the AA thing," Hank said. "Haven't seen the need in the last few years, but it was a lifesaver when I needed it. An old guy named Gramps took me to my first meeting. He used to say an angel saved him, and believe me, he was my angel. I still miss that old guy. He saved me more than once, I'll tell you."

"You could come with me sometime, you know."

"I know, but I don't think I'll drag my stinky old self into a room full of decent folks. I guess you could present me as an object lesson for how not to end up."

Pearl turned to face Hank and shook her head. "Hank, you're no such thing. Just the opposite. Look at all that life's thrown at you, and you got sober, stayed sober, and you're still kicking."

Hank rose to his feet and pulled his hood up. "I'm going to walk this chill off."

"I'll walk with you," Pearl said.

"I'm pretty weary," Hank said. "Think maybe I'm about to give in and give up. I don't mean start drinking again. That's all I need. If I was facing these cold nights liquored, I'd be dead already. But I'm tired, and don't know how much more fight I've got left in me."

"Don't talk like that," Pearl said, slowing her step and raising her voice a bit.

"Not much to live for as far as I can see," Hank said.

Pearl stopped and grabbed Hank's coat sleeve, a look of panic on her face. "You wouldn't do anything stupid, would ya?"

"Like kill myself, you mean?" Hank replied. "No, I wouldn't do that. Too much of my grannie's blood in me, I figure. She was the strongest woman I ever met."

Stopping at the intersection, they waited for the pedestrian light.

"I lost people that way and I never thought they were weak," Hank continued when they started walking again. "It's not fair to the folks you leave behind though. Not that I have a ream of those."

"You've got lots of folks who would miss you," Pearl said with a raised voice. "Me, for starters, as well as that young guy who works at the Imperial and that artist lady you're friends with. And you have a daughter and a grandson."

"I've given up on having them in my life, Pearl. I've been back in this damn city almost thirty-five years and we haven't reconnected yet. I figure it's what I deserve for being a shitty parent and leaving her in the first place."

Seeing the tears streaming down Hank's cheeks, Pearl reached in her pocket for a tissue and handed it to him.

"I can tell you a thing or two about being a shitty parent. None of my three kids want anything to do with me. But even if I failed at being the mother they deserved, I gave them life, and that counts for something. And no matter what, I know I still carry the love I have for them inside. You have always carried that love too."

Hank stopped, blew his nose, then walked over to the garbage can.

"I'm certainly not the one to give advice," Pearl said. "But it seems to me as long as you're still breathing you've got a chance to make amends with your daughter."

"I guess you're right. What makes you so smart?"

"It's the company I keep. Now how about we slip in out of this cold and get a bite to eat?"

1991

ank had been at Lone Water Farm two days before he had any direct interaction with the tall, scruffy man who always seemed to be complaining to someone about something. It seemed like the welcome talk they were all given on their first day had gone right over this guy's head. Cooperation, teamwork, and positivity were not the goals this guy seemed to be striving for. Hank had been under the impression that failure to comply would result in removal, but clearly one could be an asshole and not be asked to leave.

"This shit looks worse than the slop I fed the pigs this morning," the man grumbled as he set his plate on the tray.

"Looks better than anything I'd be cooking for myself," Hank replied.

"That's the attitude they're counting on. 'Feed these poor old sods anything. It's better than what they're used to.' Bullshit. Some of us know good food when we see it and can even throw together something a lot more edible than this disgusting mush."

Hank poured his drink and picked up his cutlery before making his way across the dining hall, hoping to be out of earshot of the rest of this guy's ranting. Instead, the man followed him and sat down at the same table.

"Mind if I sit here? The name's Russell."

"Hi, Russell. I'm Hank."

December 14, 2021

Jenny followed behind the woman as she gave her a tour of the facility. The ambulance had arrived with her mom minutes earlier, and the nurses were settling her into her room. The Bobby's Hospice building, a converted convent, was nicely decorated and homey. The palliative floor had been a step up from the regular ward, but this place seemed so much warmer and more inviting.

"We are here for the patient and the family. You are welcome to come as often as you wish and stay for as long as you like. When I'm done the tour, I'll explain the procedure for admittance if you come in after regular hours. This is the common room, and you are more than welcome to use the appliances and the space. Sometimes you just need a short break from your loved one's bedside, and you can make yourself at home here. You're welcome to bring food in. Just label it and put it in the cupboards or the fridge. People often bring treats in for everyone to share and leave them on this counter."

Passing by the open door of one of the residents' rooms Jenny recognized the song playing. Tears streamed down her cheeks as she recalled putting the Mamas & the Papas album on the turntable of the stereo in the living room years ago. That song had held such magic and mystery, connecting her to the father she could vaguely remember.

"California Dreamin'" always made her imagine her father somewhere in California, a world away to a little girl living in Sussex, New Brunswick. Did he remember holding his arms out and scooping her up as she ran to him? Did he think about her as often as she thought about him? She was a sixty-two-year-old woman. Her days of running into her father's arms were long gone, so why did this song still make her cry?

"I know these are difficult days, Mrs. Lowman. We're here to help you through them as best we can."

"I'm not a Mrs.," Jenny said, not sure why clarifying that felt important. "Just Jenny would be great."

1991

H ank wheeled the shopping cart up and down the aisles of the west side Dominion Store. Russell had given him a list, but he wasn't doing so great finding everything. He could find cans of Graves baked beans and packages of hotdogs any day, but Russell's culinary skills far exceeded that. He and Russell had moved in together three months ago, and Hank's waistline was evidence of just what a great cook Russell was.

Hank thought back to his first impressions of Russell Taylor. If people had told him in those early days that he would be in a relationship and renting an apartment with him on the west side of Saint John weeks after leaving Lone Water, he would have laughed in their faces. Laughed, or vehemently said they were full of shit.

It had taken a couple of weeks to even realize Russell was gay, but looking back, Hank recognized the anger and negativity as familiar traits he'd seen in many men who had spent years in the closet. Russell had come out several years before, but the pent-up frustration, guilt, and rage had imprinted his persona and fuelled his alcohol addiction. Chipping that away was not for the faint of heart. Why Hank had agreed to take on that challenge still puzzled him.

He hadn't been looking for a relationship, but financially it made sense to share living costs, especially since Hank had no desire to return to the rooming house. Russell was a west sider and had an uncle who owned an apartment building very near to where Hank's grandmother had lived. That was a plus, along with Hank having landed a job at the Bowlarama. Apparently, the reference from his last employer had provided enough positive comments to convince the manager that Hank Lowman was qualified to sweep and mop the floors, keep the washrooms clean, and sanitize the bowling shoes after usage.

Soya sauce, water chestnuts, peanut oil, monosodium glutamate.

Dear God, next time Russell could do his own shopping. Chicken breasts, Hank understood. He lifted a package from the cooler and placed it in his cart. He'd have to get some help finding the other items. His first shift at the Bowlarama was tonight, so he wouldn't get to eat the dish Russell was cooking up until after he got off at ten. Admittedly, the thought of that was enticing. And overall, being with Russell was a lot better than being alone.

December 15, 2021

*B*ruce had been the first to arrive with a truckload of all the parapher-nalia to deck out the square for the season just after Remembrance Day. He'd lifted the large metal trees out of the back one at a time, setting them on the trolley. But he had let the young guys do the lifting and climb-ing required to put the trees on the lamp posts and string the lights on the bandstand.

Now, walking through the square at dusk just ten days before Christ-mas as each light twinkled, Bruce felt a sense of pride, even if he'd only supervised the installation. *Christmas with Matt Anderson* lit up the mar-quee across the street, another sign of the season.

Bruce had never considered himself a Grinch, but it was hard to mus-ter up excitement for the season after Edna had declared that this year because of COVID, he wouldn't be welcome to come on Christmas Eve to see the grandkids.

"David is immune compromised," she explained. "His health is fragile and I won't expose him to someone who's out and about."

That's what you get for choosing an old man for your second husband, Bruce had wanted to fire back. *And don't you think the grandkids are around germs going to school every day?* But instead, Bruce had pleasant-ly accepted her reasoning. "Can't be too careful."

1993

H ank could feel a migraine coming on. The headaches had been more frequent than usual, and Russell thought that might be because of the fluorescent lighting and the constant noise in the bowling alley. Saturdays were always busy, but today there were more birthday parties booked than usual. Nothing like a gaggle of kids screaming and bouncing around to escalate a migraine.

Hank pushed the bucket into the men's washroom and started mopping, trying to ignore his throbbing temples and the onset of the flashes of light that always accompanied his migraines. He'd clean both washrooms and make sure there was a good assortment of sanitized footwear ready for the onslaught of birthday revellers before asking Thomas if he could take the rest of the day off. He'd lose half a day's pay, but getting home to a dark room was the only way to get rid of this headache. Soon his speech would slur, and who wants a man who seems to be drunk waiting on excited children and their anxious mothers? The high school kids who worked Saturdays could manage the afternoon without him.

::

Jenny Davis pulled the van into the parking lot of the Bowlarama. The drive from Hampton had been noisy. She'd squeezed as many little boys into her vehicle as legally possible and asked Vicki to bring in a carload as well. Ryan had invited ten kids to his birthday party, taking full advantage of her rule of having as many kids as the age you're turning. Whose dumb rule was that, anyway, and why had she thought bowling would be easier than a party at home? This was likely to be a costly and exhausting afternoon.

As Hank approached the door, he was almost knocked over by a rowdy group of boys rushing through. The mother of the birthday boy, loaded down with balloons, a cake, and several wrapped presents, was lagging a distance behind.

"Can I help you with any of that?" Hank asked.

"I should have my head examined," the woman said. "'It'll be fun. Have the party at the Bowlarama,' they said. 'No fuss, no mess. It's all done for you. Pay for a string of bowling, fill them up with pop and hotdogs, and just bring a cake. Leave the mess and cleanup behind.' Seems like a sure way to a migraine in my opinion."

Hank chuckled as he held open the door. "Have fun, ma'am!"

December 16, 2021

Stepping out of the doors of the Imperial, Liam glanced down the street and caught sight of Hank in front of the Loyalist Burial Ground, waiting to cross. He was pushing a bulging shopping cart. Hank's face seemed contorted with anger or pain. Liam quickly crossed the street and headed through the square to meet Hank.

"The bastards came this morning," Hank said when he saw Liam approach. "Pulled two fire trucks, a rescue vehicle, and a city dump truck up and just started ripping it down. An eyesore, they called it. One burly guy started firing everything into the back of the dump truck, swearing and cursing, paying no mind to my protests. He flung my tarp in first, but I managed to save this cart and a few of my things."

Liam helped Hank manoeuvre the shopping cart down off the curb and across the street. "Oh my god, Hank," he said. "Was that your place on the causeway? I just noticed it on the bank a few days ago. I saw trucks there when I came into work this morning and figured they were there to dismantle some poor bastard's home. I had no idea that that's where you've been living."

"Yeah, I'm the poor bastard and it was my home," Hank said, his breathing becoming accelerated and his balance faltering.

Liam grabbed Hank's arm to steady him and took over pushing the cart until they got to the bench and sat down.

"Try to calm yourself. Deep breaths. You're okay."

Hank's breathing quieted. He lowered his head into his hands. "I built it a way down on the bank, keeping it out of sight and out of the wind. But not out of sight enough, I guess," he said, his words muffled.

Liam put his arm around Hank.

"An eyesore," Hank exclaimed, jumping to his feet. "They called it an eyesore. Jesus Christ, what about that garbage dump on the hill beside the old dome of the General? That looks a lot worse than a blue tarp down over the bank of the causeway. I never threw one piece of garbage around my place. And if nothing else they could have asked nicely for me to move it. And they just chucked a perfectly good mattress in with everything else. Sorry, Liam. I'm a little wound up."

"I don't blame you, Hank. That's terrible. What are you going to do now?" he asked gently after a few seconds of silence.

"Look for another spot, I guess. Maybe if I find good tree cover somewhere, it might be a while before folks notice and start complaining."

"I thought all along that you were in a rooming house," Liam said.

"I was, but it got sold a few weeks ago. They're turning the building into high-end condos, but as far as I can tell they haven't even started working on the renovations. Something like that godawful hole where Woolworths used to be. Not a thing going on there yet."

"I know. Seems like things are at a standstill everywhere. No workers and a major supply chain problem, they say. So many buildings just sitting empty and guys like you with nowhere to live. It's not right."

"You're damn right it's not. They could have let us stay until spring at least." Hank gestured across the street at the marquee. "That Newfie guy comes tonight, right? Don't let my troubles keep ya from having your lunch break."

"I do have to get back, but take my lunch, would you please? Amanda would have a fit if she thought it didn't get eaten," Liam said.

"Thanks. You're a good kid, Liam. Meet me here tomorrow and you can tell me how tonight went. Don't fret about me. I'll be fine."

"You could come over this afternoon and give us a hand unloading equipment. It would give you a few hours out of the cold, some bad coffee, and a few bucks."

"Yeah, I could do that, but I've got to find somewhere to stash this cart. Some heavy blankets and a plastic sheet are valuable, and there's lots who'd be happy to snatch them up."

"I can take it and stick it in the storeroom for now. The trucks are supposed to arrive at two o'clock. They'll pull in off Charlotte. Come around to the loading door and I'll let you in. Wait until I tell the guys we've got Hank Lowman helping today. I've told them all about you."

"I'll keep my eyes peeled for it and come over when I see it pull up. Thank you."

1994

H ank hung up his wet coat and slipped into the back of the meeting room at the Hillcrest Baptist Church.

"I'm not going out in that pouring rain," Russell had hollered after him as he was leaving the apartment.

Hank had almost hurled back the angry accusation that the rain had nothing to do with him not going to tonight's meeting. Russell hadn't been to a meeting in months and he wasn't fooling Hank with his angry claim of staying sober "without any goddamn meetings." But instead of a confrontation Hank had left quickly, silently reciting AA's three Cs: *I didn't cause it; I can't control it, and I can't cure it.*

Hank took a deep breath and looked around the room quickly. One of the regulars stood to address the room.

"I'm sorry to inform you tonight that we've lost a long-time member and a good friend."

Hank felt a panic rise in his throat waiting for the man to continue.

"I just got word before the meeting that Archie Higgins passed away."

Audible gasps rippled through the room. Some members reached out, offering support to the person next to them. There probably wasn't a person in this room that hadn't had some interaction with Gramps. This wasn't his home group, but he'd encouraged just about everyone in this room at one time or another and had possibly been pivotal in convincing a good number of them to seek recovery.

1996

"Where is my blue shirt?" Russell asked.

"In the closet, I assume," Hank replied. "When's the last time you wore it?"

"How the hell would I know? You wear my shirts all the time."

"Calm down. Take your time and look for it."

"Can you imagine how Carl and Jim are feeling if the two of us are in such a tizzy getting ready?" Russell said, pulling the blue shirt from the hanger.

"I'm not in a tizzy," Hank said. "In case you haven't noticed, I've been ready for an hour. We're going to have to take a cab if we want to be on time. It's too late to catch the bus over."

Russell moved toward the dresser, buttoning his shirt and tucking it in to his pants. He pulled a tie from the top drawer. "How many did they invite?"

"I'm not sure, but I expect there will be a bigger crowd than just their friends. This is huge, you know. The first same-sex union to be conducted in a church, in the Maritimes anyway. Lots of shit hitting the fan. They've gotten threats. I expect there will be lots of protesters outside the church. Who knows what will happen? Let's get going. The least we can do is get there on time and show our support."

"I suppose you'll be starting your Harvey Milk spiel, Hank. Things are never going to change. It's one thing to come out, but we're just asking for trouble parading our relationships in front of the public."

"They'll never change with attitudes like yours. Surely to God it has to start with us being brave enough to expect the right to be who we are."

"Next thing you'll be wanting to traipse down the aisle and marry me," Russell said.

Hank pulled on his sports jacket. A lump in his throat prevented a response. Marvin had been in his waking and sleeping thoughts for weeks, since Jim and Carl had told him of their plans for today's covenanting ceremony. He'd also wondered what George would say if he were alive to witness this day. And would Raphael have made the decision he made if he had been legally able to claim Roberto as his husband?

"I'm going outside to wait for the cab," Hank said.

"Maybe I won't even bother going," Russell yelled across the room. "Those people are all your friends, not mine. I'm not sure why you're even still here."

Hank slammed the door, choking back his anger and frustration. Why *was* he still here?

1999

H ank walked through the doors of the church and was overwhelmed seeing the packed boxes and furniture in the foyer. He knew moving day would not be easy, but he hadn't been prepared for just how hard it was to accept. Being a part of the congregation at Centenary Queen Square United Church had become such an important part of his life. That would continue in the storefront space the church was moving into, but leaving this beautiful old building was heartbreaking.

"Good morning, Hank," Pastor Johnston said. "You by yourself?"

Russell had stopped coming with Hank long ago, but people still asked after him every time. And every time, Hank gave some excuse for being alone. But he'd long given up believing any of Russell's excuses and was only concentrating on maintaining his own recovery. Weekly meetings and being a part of this church family were an important part of that. Having a place to live he could afford and that was close to work were reasons enough to stay with Russell. Hank had never expected more.

"Yeah. Russell's working. Does it matter where I start?" Hank asked.

"This all has to go. Just start grabbing whatever you can carry. Tom and Harold left and Dorothy is going to stay on Wentworth while the rest of us do the heavy lifting. She came ready to help, but I convinced her we needed somebody to stay behind and open the doors for the rest of us. God love her."

Dorothy Miller had been such a good friend to Hank since the first day he'd walked through the church doors. She sat down beside him that day and for some reason she took a liking to him. The eighty-six-year-old woman was a force to reckon with. She had more energy than most people half her age and was always smiling. She dressed in bright, colourful clothes and kept her white hair streaked with rainbow colours. Every

Sunday, Dorothy drove out of her way to pick Hank up for the morning service.

"God love her, all right," Hank said, picking up a large box and heading out the door.

December 16, 2021

H ank left the Imperial just as it was coming on dark. It had felt so good to be helping out, and as the sound checks and warmup began, he felt the same adrenalin he'd always felt at the soundboard. No one seemed bothered that some strange old man was helping set up, and Liam seemed genuinely pleased to be able to introduce him to his coworkers. After this morning's upset it had been a great afternoon, and the money Liam had passed him minutes ago was more than generous. It was enough to pay for a night in a warm room at the hotel on City Road. He wouldn't try any of the fancier ones. A shower would be amazing.

Hank was crossing the square when Liam ran up behind him.

"Hold up there, Hank," Liam called out. "I don't think they'll take cash. I was telling Scott about you heading to the Day's Inn and he said he was pretty sure they only accept credit cards."

Hank leaned up against the bandstand, letting Liam's words sink in. He felt the anger and frustration that he'd been able to keep at bay all afternoon, thanks to Liam. The last thing he wanted was to blow up and appear ungrateful. "Well, I was really looking forward to having a shower and sleeping in a comfy bed. Doesn't seem right that cash is no good. It's not your fault, son."

"I feel terrible. If I had time, I'd take you there and put it on my credit card, but I've got to get back. I didn't want you walking all the way to City Road and the bastards not let you have a room."

"You know the hardest part of all this?" Hank said, emotion rising in his voice. "The shittiest part, really. I'm sure not many people even think about it. But it's taking a shit."

Liam heard the vulnerability in Hank's words and said nothing, waiting for Hank to continue.

"'Everybody shits,' my father used to say," Hank continued. "And that is the truth of it. But most folks get to shit in the comfort of their own bathroom. I was really looking forward to a bathroom for my morning shit tomorrow. I am so damn tired of employing the poop-and-scoop method like a good dog owner."

"I'm so sorry, Hank," Liam said.

"Not your fault, son," Hank repeated. "Thanks for coming to find me."

"What are you going to do?"

"I'm going to go have a good sit-down meal and then I'll see if I can get into the shelter for the night. Things will look up tomorrow. You get back to work. And thanks."

"Do you want your cart?"

"No, I'll come by tomorrow and get it once I figure out where I'm going to go. Don't you worry about me."

Hank walked back through the square and crossed Charlotte Street. The girls at the Uptown Pub Down Under would serve him up a good supper. They let him eat there sometimes, even when he didn't have quite enough to cover the bill. Tonight, he'd leave them a good tip.

Hank turned on to Germain to escape the bitter wind. He could see that Gloria's light was still on. He'd stop in and offer to buy her supper if she wasn't in a hurry to get home.

"You're staying late tonight, Gloria," Hank said as she opened the door.

"Ted's curling tonight, so I thought I'd stay later and work on a commission. It's a big piece, and I'd like to get it finished soon so I can get back to the ones I enjoy doing. Not sure why I take special orders. I'd rather paint what suits my fancy than what someone else wants. What have you been up to today?"

"Well, it's been a day of ups and downs. I made a bit of money, though, and I'll treat you to supper if you'll take a break."

"That would be great. I was just thinking I was getting a bit peckish. Come inside while I clean up my brushes and get ready to go."

Hank slipped off his boots and followed Gloria into her studio. Sitting down, he realized just how weary he was, and how much of a toll this morning's incident had taken on him. He closed his eyes, enjoying the heat of the room as Gloria scurried around cleaning up.

"Okay, I'm ready," Gloria said. "I think you were snoozing. Where will we go?"

"How about the Down Under place on Prince William?" Hank answered. "They do a great fish and chips, but you can have anything you'd like."

"Sounds great, and you can tell me more about your up-and-down day. Kind of had one of those myself."

2003

Hank turned the radio up, not sure why he was making himself listen to the rant again. All day, each hour, clips from Elsie Wayne's speech in parliament had topped CHSJ's news reports. Elsie Wayne had even been on *The National* last night, and at first he and Russell had been quite excited to see the mayor of their own city on the national news. But the hurtful words she'd hurled and the follow-up interview defending her stand against gays and lesbians had quickly changed Hank's feelings.

"If they are going to live together, they can go live together and shut up about it."

A short quote had been in the previous clips, but the longer, more accusatory part of the rant had been added this time. Russell came into the kitchen just as Elsie was getting wound up.

"Why do they have to be out there in the public always debating that they want to call it marriage? Why are they in the parades? Why are they dressed up as women on floats? Why do they have to go around trying to get a whole lot of publicity?"

"I told you we were just asking for trouble," Russell said. "Ceremonies like Carl and Jim's and all the publicity around that have just fuelled the fire. And that pride parade Judith and Wayne are cooking up is going to stir up more hatred. What makes you think anyone gives a shit about our rights? We're better off shutting up about it, like Elsie says."

Hank turned the radio off and walked over to the stove. Picking up the wooden spoon, he stirred the simmering pot of chili. "Is this ready?"

"Yeah, it's ready, I guess," Russell answered. "You asked me to make chili so I made chili."

"Are you sure you won't come to the potluck, Russell?" Hank asked.

"I had my fill of being dragged off to church when I was a kid," Russell said. "You think all those phonies give a shit about us? They just want money, same as every other church."

Hank left the kitchen in frustration. It seemed these days he was always on the verge of flying into a rage or collapsing into tears. But he wouldn't do either. He would instead carry the pot of chili out to the front step and wait for Dorothy to pick him up. She would greet him with a big smile and lift his spirits.

December 16, 2021

wo hours passed quickly as Hank and Gloria ate supper and talked. Hank told her about the early morning destruction of his shelter and Gloria told him about the fight she and Ted had had that morning.

"Why are you fighting over me?" Hank quipped. "You don't owe me anything, Gloria, and I'm sure as hell not worth losing your husband over."

"We've been through worse than this," Gloria said. "I just don't get why he won't see my point of view. We've got the space. He'll come around, I'm sure, but for now you're staying in the studio. That old couch isn't the best, but it's comfortable. And there's lots of hot water, even if there isn't a shower."

Hank stared across the table, taken aback by Gloria's suggestion. He should have left at least an hour ago if he hoped to get a bed in the shelter tonight, but he'd tell her he had a place to go so she wouldn't feel obligated to follow through with the offer she'd just made.

"Gloria, I didn't tell you my sad story so you'd feel sorry for me."

"You're staying in the studio until I can convince Ted to let you come to our place, for the winter at least. He has known me long enough to know that when I make up my mind there's no stopping me."

Hank thought back to the comfort he'd felt dozing off while waiting for Gloria earlier. How wonderful would it be to actually sleep all night on her couch, warm and safe under a roof? Maybe he could accept her generosity for tonight and see what options he might have tomorrow.

"Okay, I'll sleep in your studio tonight," Hank said. "I've only known you a short time, but I can already see you might have a stubborn streak."

::

"I'm stuffed," Gloria said as she and Hank walked out on to the street. "And so much for getting any painting done tonight, Hank. You're a bad influence on me."

"What year did you say you left and came to live in the city?" Hank asked as they rounded the corner.

"It was 2013," Gloria answered. "God, time flies by, but some years stand out."

"You're right about that," Hank said. "Actually, 2013 was quite a memorable year for me too. It was a rough one. Spent some time in the psych ward. Probably shouldn't tell you that. It might change your mind about letting me stay in the studio, and for sure about letting me into your home."

"I have no reservations about letting you stay here. And it's none of my business what happened that year unless you want to tell me," Gloria said as she unlocked the door and passed Hank the key. "I've got another key at home."

"I don't need a key, Gloria. You'll be here in the morning, won't you?"

"Yes, but as far as I'm concerned you are staying here until I can convince Ted to let you move in with us for the winter at least. So, if you have a key you can come and go as you please. I keep blankets, towels, and facecloths in the bathroom closet in case I'm ever storm stayed, so help yourself. I'll see you in the morning. Goodnight, Hank."

2013

Hank turned the volume up and moved closer to the small TV screen. California had issued the first marriage licence to a same-sex couple yesterday, Kristin Perry and Sandra Stier, after the Ninth Circuit stay had been lifted. Many couples followed suit and were married that day.

Hank focused intently on the news story. This was what he and Marvin had dreamed of when Harvey Milk was organizing rallies in San Francisco for the legalization of same-sex marriage. This is why over two hundred people had gathered in Queen's Square on July 26, 2003, for Saint John's first Pride Parade supporting equal rights for gays and lesbians. This is what the four same-sex couples who filed a court challenge in New Brunswick in 2005 had believed in.

"We're going to walk down the aisle someday, Canada," Marvin had said the first night he told Hank he loved him. "Harvey is paving the way for us. It's no mystery who'll wear the white dress and veil, is it, darling? Although I'd wear a paper bag to stand beside you and legally claim you as my husband."

Thirty-six years it had taken California to realize Harvey Milk's vision of equality. Too late for Harvey, and too late for Marvin.

"I don't care what the law says, Canada. You are my husband."

Hank walked over and punched his fist into the wall at the far end of the room. He flinched and hit it the second time. He gasped as the sobbing began. He slumped to the floor and let the emotion crest.

2013

*L*ooking out her window, Gloria watched the rain dancing off the sidewalk. Water was pooling near the stop sign, car tires splashing through the already deep puddle. Gloria could only imagine how muddy the pig yard was at the farm and how much of the steep driveway would already be washed out. Waking up in the city still took her by surprise most mornings, and in the middle of night the glare of the streetlights streaming through the blinds often confused her.

It had been four months since she'd driven down the long lane, a teary mess fuelled by the collapse of her carefully constructed emotional barricade. She hadn't started the day knowing she would leave, but as she drove away, she knew she wasn't coming back anytime soon. The relief she felt had been immediate and she quickly put her energies into her relocation plans.

Germain Street had been her threat for the last few years whenever she and Ted fought. *When push comes to shove, I'll look after myself and I'll move to Germain Street.* When push comes to shove; a funny saying, really. There had never been pushing, shoving, or any physical altercations. They hardly ever fought, rarely raised their voices to one another, but maybe that had been part of the problem.

Non-confrontational, a pushover, a wimp, passive aggressive, all terms Gloria used to describe herself, and in the long run those traits hadn't really gotten her anywhere. Forty years of marriage—not all bad, of course, and the one constant causing most of the pain. Burying their oldest son had made all the other pain dull and easy to dismiss. All the pain in one messy big ball of string, not easy to unravel and seemingly best left tangled and unaddressed. But she'd spent the last four months facing the problem head on, untangling it one day at a time.

SUSAN WHITE

Of course, Ted was surprised, the grandkids bewildered, and her adult children worried and shocked. But no one was as surprised as she herself had been. What made the day she left any different from all the other days she'd escaped up the wood road hill, allowing her sadness and fear to cascade out in sobs, prayers, and screaming pleas to God? Sometimes she'd call out to her dead parents, sing remembered hymns at the top of her lungs, and wait for the open sky to quiet her turmoil. She had always rallied and come back home to keep doing what she'd been doing for years.

It was Princess Street, not Germain after all, that had provided the escape she'd driven toward in June, and despite the constant tug to go home, this street-level window was the perspective she took comfort in on this day, one month before her sixtieth birthday. Not the teenager who moved into her first apartment two blocks away, but a grown woman desperate for the freedom, independence, and hope she'd felt back then.

2013

Hank squinted in the bright sunshine. This morning's release had come as a bit of a surprise. Apparently, he wasn't top priority on the crazy scale, and someone crazier needed his bed on 3D North. "An outpatient plan," the doctor called it. A cab would come by, pick him up, and take him to the Salvation Army shelter. Once a week he'd be required to meet with his social worker and see the psychiatrist monthly.

A psychotic breakdown, they called it. Russell's uncle hadn't pressed charges for the damage Hank had done to the City Line apartment in the throes of that breakdown but was unwilling to have him return. Hank was more than happy to avoid the west side anyway and had no plans to go back to the Bowlarama even if he still had a job. Crossing the Reversing Falls bridge or even seeing it from a distance was too much. Would visions of Russell climbing over the railing and dropping into the roiling water below ever leave him? Not that he had actually seen it, but eye witness accounts were enough to give him a clear picture.

Had Hank done enough to prevent it? The question haunted him. Should he have known that morning that Russell was thinking of suicide? He'd been upset for weeks over his son's refusal to see him. Had Hank made it worse with his own obsession to find Jennifer? His last trip to Hampton had been another dead end. The bungalow he'd gone to years before now had a *For Sale* sign on the lawn and a neighbour had told him of the Davises' divorce. Failing yet again, decades after returning to the city, had put Hank in a funk and he'd had no patience or sympathy to offer Russell.

The truth of it was that Hank had been watching Russell's downward spiral for much longer than the last few weeks. For his own selfish reasons, he'd stayed even when Russell started drinking again and became harder to get along with. With them both working and Hank's church involvement, they spent very little time at home together, and the arrangement seemed to serve them both. But after City Laundry closed, putting Russell out of work, things got even worse. And then Hank stopped attending church when Dorothy went into Rocmaura Nursing Home.

The doctor kept telling him he was not responsible for Russell's death, but Hank kept silent, knowing his reaction to Russell's death was about so much more. When he'd been told about it, Hank immediately went to thoughts of George struggling in the deep water, and the brutal attack on Marvin. Of course, he was sorry Russell had killed himself, but this loss only served to bring up the excruciating core of pain he felt over George's death and losing Marvin. It was the inability to push that pain back down that triggered his breakdown.

A month in hospital hadn't done much to quell that pain, but Hank was determined to endure it without going back to the bottle and without returning to meetings. Gramps's voice still echoed in his head and that would be enough AA for him. He had no interest in trying to fit back into the church community and he certainly would not look for another relationship. For now, he would keep to himself and do the best he could to tackle each day as it came.

December 17, 2021

Jenny pulled her car over, letting the impact of the call she'd just received register. How unfair it was that after she'd sat by her mother's bedside day after day, her mother's last breath came when her daughter was only minutes away from arriving at the west side building. Her rational mind knew that in the end it made no difference. Yesterday her mother hadn't even opened her eyes, and there had been no conscious interaction for over a week.

The nurses and staff at Bobby's Hospice were sweet and had offered so much comfort. They said caring and compassionate things, but their words carried some mixed messages. *Sometimes they wait for their loved ones to leave before passing. They know you are in the room. If you take a break, you have nothing to feel guilty about. You have done all you can do. Being present as they take their last breath is a wonderful gift. You need to go home and have a good night's sleep.*

Jenny wiped her tears and pulled back out on to the road. She'd known this day would come, so on she'd go. She had done the best she could. The woman who called said her mother's body would still be in the room for her to say her goodbyes. Arrangements were in place, the obituary written with only the dates to be added. She would call Ryan so he and Serge could make flight plans. Maybe they would even consider staying for Christmas.

Sometimes they have perfect timing. It is not for us to understand. In God's time, not ours. The strength you have been given thus far will still be enough to get you through her passing. Every cloud has a silver lining.

2014

Walking into the room, Hank stood to look out the window before sitting down. He could see the red Salvation Army shield fixed to the side of the brick building. Rumours were running rampant that the place he'd called home since leaving the hospital several months ago was struggling to stay open.

Darcy Jacobs walked in, her smile and optimism radiating as usual. She passed Hank a large Tim Hortons coffee. "Good morning, Mr. Lowman."

"What's with this Mr. Lowman shit? Thanks for the coffee, Darce."

"Just how you like it, Hank. Three sugars, as if you aren't sweet enough."

Hank and Darcy sat down at the round table. Darcy reached into her leather bag and pulled out a file folder. Hank could see his name on the tab.

"This place is closing at the end of April, Hank. We need to find you alternate housing before that happens."

Hank looked across the table at his social worker. This meeting was the highlight of his week. Sometimes he imagined Darcy Jacobs was Jennifer, even though the ages didn't match. He never said that out loud, of course. But fantasy and made-up internal dialogue seemed to be getting him through the days. The nights were another story. He woke in the grips of troublesome dreams, struggling to regain some calm from his panic and despair. But at least most days he was able to put on good face.

"Dr. Fowler thinks I need a job," Hank said. "Not sure who he thinks is going to hire a crazy old coot like me."

"The rooming house I called yesterday said maybe if you were willing you could do some odd jobs and that could go toward your rent. They want some painting done, the garbage collected, and maintenance when it comes up. Kind of a super's job helping to keep the place in order. Is that something you might be interested in?"

"Yeah, I guess so. I owned a house once and I was the handyman, not Marvin. He had the decorating flare though. Where is this place? Not the west side, is it?"

"No, it's on Duke in the south end. Not a bad place. The building is in decent shape and the owner vets everyone. He has a no-drug, no-alcohol policy, which cuts down on the trouble. There's a common room and kitchen in the basement where residents can cook their own meals if they clean up after themselves. It's the best place I could find, and with the extra offer thrown in I think it would be perfect for you."

"Well, who I am to argue with that? When can I move in?"

"The room's yours at the first of March. You'll need a bed and a dresser. I think I can get donations and get you set up."

"Thanks, Darcy. I really appreciate all you've done for me."

2015

H ank lifted the mop, wringing it out into the bucket. Since the addition of the Sony flat screen in the common room, it seemed he had to clean this floor more often. Grown men were as messy as a bunch of kids. This evening's challenge was a spot where someone had spilled a can of Coke earlier and not bothered to even soak it up. The August heat had made it a sticky mess.

Hank ran the mop over the floor again, then sat himself down to let the floor dry before putting all the furniture back in place. He reached for the remote and turned on the CBC news. It wasn't often he had any choice of channels as it always seemed someone else was watching first.

Hank was almost dozing off when the word *gay* caught his attention. Close-up photographs of two young men caused him to move closer to the screen. As pages of an old photograph album were turned, the announcer said "lesbian, gay, bisexual, transgender, and queer" and mentioned something called the New Brunswick Queer initiative.

The young man on the screen was now talking about a photograph of a row of men in a POW camp in Amherst, Nova Scotia. He commented on the fact that the men were dressed in drag. One smiling man in a dress and wearing a mop wig made Hank think of Marvin's gorgeous dresses and striking wigs.

A photograph of two shirtless young men in an embrace brought a flood of emotion and Hank turned up the volume. The photographs were from 1915 and belonged to a man named Leonard Keith. Dozens more photographs showed Keith and his boyfriend, Cub Coates, at their cabin outside of Havelock. The announcer said they spent two years together, but their time at the cabin came to a sudden end.

Tears filled Hank's eyes as he thought back to the sudden end of the time he and Marvin had together in their home.

"They were eventually outed and driven out of Havelock. Rural New Brunswick in the 1920s was not a good time to be gay," the young man said, before adding that he too had grown up gay in rural New Brunswick.

"What are you watching?" Donnie Steeves said, plopping himself down on the couch beside Hank. "And who the hell are those fags?"

Hank got up and started putting everything back in order. He then picked up the mop and pail and left the room, resisting the urge to empty the dirty water over Donnie's head.

Being gay in 2015 was no walk in the park either, Hank thought as he stomped up the stairs.

December 20, 2021

H ank held the door open as Gloria squeezed the short, bushy tree into the hallway. Closing the door, he helped her stand it upright.

"You weren't kidding," Hank said. "You got a tree. Not sure why you're bothering. Not just for me, I hope."

"You have to have a tree, Hank. I feel terrible not being able to have you come to our house for Christmas."

"Don't be ridiculous. You're having a houseful, and the last thing you need is to spring an old homeless guy on everyone."

"That's the meaning of the season as far as I'm concerned. Can't believe I'm using the *no room at the inn* excuse. But with all the kids, grandkids, and Ted's sister and her husband, we really *don't* have any room at the inn. But I'm going to decorate this little tree and leave you a few presents to open Christmas day. I bought you some groceries, too."

"You are too good to me. Have you got a stand to put it in?"

"It's out in the trunk along with the lights and some ornaments. I even brought you in a stocking to hang."

2016

"What the hell is Facebook?" Hank asked.

Darcy Jacobs pushed her laptop over, showing Hank her profile page. "It's called social media, and it's the way a lot of people stay connected these days. I could probably search Jennifer Davis and find your daughter's profile page. You'd be surprised at what you can find out from a person's photos and posts."

"Isn't that a bit creepy, going on and looking at other people's pictures?" Hank said.

"I just thought it might help you connect with your daughter," Darcy said.

"Well, that's kind of you, Darcy, but I'd rather you didn't," Hank said. "I've accepted the fact that getting to know my daughter is never going to happen. Why the hell would she want to have me in her life?" Hank stood up and started sweeping the common room floor.

"I think she'd be lucky to have you, Hank," Darcy said, hopping up to move the chairs from around the table. "I'm going to miss our sessions."

"Don't be so silly. You deserve that promotion, and now you won't have to put up with messed-up old guys like me. I'm not too keen on getting used to a new worker though."

"There's not a thing messed up about you, and it's been no trouble having you on my caseload," Darcy said, putting her hand on Hank's shoulder. "You've done so well that Social Services isn't assigning another worker. I'm really proud of you. And you're not getting rid of me that easy. I won't be your social worker, but I'll always be your friend."

2018

"Why would you want an old coot like me at your wedding?" Hank asked.

Hank had finished his dessert and second cup of coffee when Darcy passed him the envelope. She'd said nothing during their lunch date, and the contents of the envelope took Hank by surprise.

"I don't have any family in the city, Hank, and believe it or not, I think of you like a grandfather."

"Pretty hard up, aren't you, if you have to pick a stand-in family from your list of past lost causes."

"You know I never considered you a lost cause."

"Not too sure you're a good judge of character, then. Who's this guy you're marrying in such a hurry?"

"It's a woman, actually, and we've been together for five years. You met Hilary at Christmastime."

"You're marrying Hilary? Well, I'll be. I thought I had an eye for that sort of thing."

"And what sort of thing is that?" Darcy laughed. "It's at 23 Orange Street, three o'clock on Saturday afternoon."

"Can I bring anything?"

"Just yourself. We're going to order from Julius Pizza after the ceremony."

December 22, 2021

It was just by chance that Hank saw the Obituary section of the December 21 *Telegraph Journal*. Gloria had brought the newspaper in from home, thinking he'd be interested. Not much in it, really, and no good news. But because she bothered, Hank skimmed through it as Gloria got her paints laid out for the day.

"I'm starting a painting of the Gothic Arches today, Hank. What a shame so many of this city's treasures have been demolished. The list is long, starting with the old Union Station. And I cried the day they tore down the jellybean houses."

"I had friends say their vows at the Gothic Arches. Russell and I were invited to the ceremony. Most of the gay community gathered to celebrate that monumental day. Lots of protest too, though. Good church folk horrified that two queers were being joined together in a house of the Lord."

Hank read through the obituary again. Tanya was dead. Her funeral was at eleven o'clock today, a block down the street at Trinity. He wasn't bold enough to think he had any right to attend. He'd pay his respects from a distance, maybe from the sidewalk across the street. Watching people enter, maybe he'd be able to figure out which one was Jennifer. Family would arrive together, no doubt, and he might even get a glimpse of his grandson.

"Jennifer's mother died," Hank said as he folded up the newspaper. "Her obit is in here. The funeral is this morning. Jennifer goes by Lowman, dropped her married name, I guess. She only had the one child, Ryan. Guess he'd be thirty-eight years old now. Lists a partner's name beside his. Serge. That's a man's name, isn't it?"

"I would think so. Are you planning to go?"

"God, no. I have no right to show up. Not the time or the place."

"How are you feeling?"

"How am I feeling about Tanya dying? Says Tanya's second husband predeceased her. No mention of me, of course. Donations to the Cancer Society. Hope she didn't suffer too long. How am I feeling about my daughter burying her mother when she never knew her father? How am I feeling about my grandson maybe being gay if Serge is a guy's name?" His voice was trembling now. "How am I feeling about being an old piece of shit who never tried hard enough to have a relationship with his only kid and his only grandkid? Not great."

2020

Hank stopped at the barricade, the strong wind hitting his face. Since early December, he'd made the trek up Wentworth every day to observe the demolition of the Centenary Queen Square United Church. The newscasts always referred to the building as the Gothic Arches, but the church he'd joined shortly after Jim and Carl's ceremony would always be Centenary Queen Square to him. The place was sacred, and the loss of it felt heavy as each day it disappeared a little more.

"Isn't it so sad watching this? What a treasure we're losing," said a woman walking up beside him. Hank recognized her as someone who came as regularly as he did to watch the demolition.

"A treasure for sure," he said. He wanted to add that more than the architecture, this building represented the courageous stand its pastor and congregation took in 1996. There had been so much fallout when they'd made the decision to conduct the first same-sex union in the Maritimes. Vandalism, protests, church members leaving in droves, and public outcry followed, which contributed to the demise of the building.

At the last service, in 1999, he had wept with many of the others. No longer could the cost of keeping up such a grand old building be met by the small congregation. He had rallied with the others to move into the rented storefront on Wentworth Street and enjoyed that fellowship until Dorothy went into care. A couple of years later the shrinking membership was unable to meet the financial demands of the rented space and people joined other congregations.

"An historic building," Hank added, closing his eyes and bowing his head briefly before turning to walk back home.

Was this daily trek really about watching the demolition, or was this ritual more about excavating his memories and heartache? Since moving into the rooming house six years ago, he'd kept busy with the job of caretaker, which gave him enough purpose to put his feet on the floor every day, stay sober, and maintain his existence, however lacklustre. He'd buried good friends like Gramps and Dorothy. He still missed Darcy; she and Hilary had moved to Halifax, though she always sent cards at Christmas and on his birthday. It felt like all the community he'd worked so hard to build up over his decades back in Saint John had slowly evaporated and left him with a tiny, solitary life. His days were predictable, though, and life was manageable.

But the nights were sometimes peppered with misery when dreams put him into the throes of Marvin's attack, on the deck of the fishing boat during George's last minutes, or on the Reversing Falls bridge watching Russell climb the railing to his death. Sometimes the dreams were calmer but filled with sightings of Jennifer. He could never catch up to her or call out loud enough for her to hear his anguished plea for forgiveness.

Watching the machinery, hearing the whir of the engines and the crash of the rubble, Hank felt a bit of his pain disperse in the dust of the debris hitting the ground. Maybe if he kept coming until every trace of the grand old structure was gone, his inner turmoil would be gone too, letting him live out whatever time he had left in a state of calm oblivion.

December 22, 2021

*D*avid Higgins hung up the phone, still registering the information the caller had relayed. How had she even gotten his phone number? He was his mother's next of kin, apparently. Well, wasn't that a hoot. At first it had taken a second to even register who Pearl Jennings was. She was on a respirator, the woman said, and not doing well, and as her next of kin it was up to him to decide if a DNR (Do Not Recessitate) should be put in place. She had to explain what DNR meant and went on to say just how fragile his mother was.

His mother had never been a big woman, but the nurse said she was seriously underweight. She had come to the hospital with breathing difficulties three days ago and her condition had quickly deteriorated. It was not likely she would recover. Another COVID statistic, David thought, even though like most people he had stopped paying attention to the case tally and death numbers. He had all his shots, but there was no way he was going into the hospital and risking infection. He'd call Kenny and Ruth first, and then maybe the DNR order could be given over the phone.

December 23, 2021

M iriam put the phone down as her boss approached her desk. Things were slow the week before Christmas, but calling clients right back was important to her. Appearing to be a loyal employee was important too, so she'd get back to the call after this conversation.

"Sorry to interrupt, Miriam, but I'm trying to line up some volunteers to serve up Christmas dinner at Romero House this year. Showing community spirit looks good for the company. I'll be making a press release later today and want to make sure I've got some agents willing to participate. I'm asking those without families first. Are you interested? Your photograph would be in the promo piece."

"What would I have to do? I don't cook."

"No cooking involved, and this year with COVID, the meals will be handed out the window instead of having the people come inside. You wouldn't even have to interact with them. You'd just have to dish up the meals, from what I understand. Maybe butter the rolls or cut the pies. Whatever the job, it looks good on us. Can I count on you?"

"Yeah, I guess so. Wouldn't take all day, would it?"

"I'll get more details and let you know what time to be there and how long you'll be expected to stay. Thanks, Miriam. I'll let you get back to work."

The agents with no families. He was right on that account. She may as well be scooping up potatoes at a soup kitchen on Christmas day instead of sitting home alone heating up a frozen dinner.

::

"There's something quite magical about this place when the bandstand is lit," Bruce said as he sat down beside Hank. "The light snowfall adds to the beauty. Even those gaudy green trees on the lampposts look nice tonight."

"Is that why you're strolling through King's Square at this time of day?" Hank asked.

"Nothing better to do, bud. To be honest with you, I've walked here every night since we put up the Christmas decorations. Not much else to do with my evenings. Let's walk to Keirstead's Flower Shop," Bruce suggested. "It's lit up real nice."

"Never took you for a romantic," Hank said.

Bruce and Hank walked a block down Charlotte and stopped to admire the display in the shop window.

"I try to find the beauty in this city wherever I can," Bruce said. "But there's lots not so beautiful, like the fact that guys like you can't find a decent place they can afford to live in."

The two men walked along Germain Street, taking in the beauty of the light snow falling on the Christmas lights trimming the doors and windows of the heritage houses.

"Where you living right now, Hank?" Bruce asked a few minutes later. "I know they took your shelter on the causeway down. I suppose they just pitched your mattress along with everything else."

"Yeah, they sure did," Hank said. "I'm staying at a friend's place, on this street actually, and I'm on a waiting list for a rooming house on Princess. Maybe 2022 will be a better year for this old guy. If I last until then, that is."

"What makes you say that? Are you sick?"

"No, I'm just old and tired. Never thought I'd make it to my eighties. Not many of us do, you know. So many obstacles preventing old age for a gay man. AIDS of course wiped so many out, but violence and suicide were other big killers. I've lost friends and lovers to all that and I'm amazed every day that I'm still here. It's not easy being the last man standing."

By this time, they had made their way back to King's Square, parking themselves on Hank's bench again.

"I think that's a wedding party," Bruce said, pointing across the square. "Looks like they're posing for pictures on the bandstand. Nice backdrop, if I do say so myself."

"You didn't string those lights, Bruce. Said you were too old for that foolishness this year."

"I supervised," Bruce said. "I set the standard, too, my friend. I've been around for a lot of Christmas light installations."

"It's two men," Hank said suddenly, rising to his feet to get a better look. "Two handsome young men hand in hand on the day of their marriage. God bless them. That makes my heart soar."

::

"Do gay guys throw their bouquets?" Ryan called out.

"Throw it to Mama," Jenny said. "Maybe it's not too late for me."

Ryan took the spray of daisies and held them high above his head, his gaze on the small crowd gathered around them. He squinted to take in the beauty of the twinkling lights in this beautiful square with the light snow covering the ground. It had been a last-minute decision to come to King's Square for pictures. Earlier they'd said their vows in front of the justice of peace and gathered for a meal at Billy's Seafood.

"I want pictures taken over there," Ryan stated. "As a little boy my Gram would take me to movies at the Paramount. Afterwards she would always walk me across the square. She'd show me the school she went to and then we'd walk by the Imperial Theatre. She always told me about the day my grandfather met her there, and they told her parents they were having Mom. 'I forgave him for leaving a long time ago,' she told me, 'and I'm so thankful he gave me you and your mother. I feel him here,' she always said."

December 24, 2021

Hank walked along Charlotte, thinking of the changes he'd seen just since returning to Saint John in 1986. Calp's was closed, the Paramount gone, and this whole block seemed dead compared to how busy it once was. Processing the changes since growing up here seemed too much to manage. Why was it that after all this time he still questioned his choice to leave? If he'd just stayed and lived the life his parents imagined for him, how different everything might have been. He'd known men over the years who did just that. They fit themselves into the slot they were expected to fill and lived the charade.

Thoughts of the gay wedding he'd seen yesterday came to mind. What a different world it was now. Of course, there was still intolerance and hatred, but two young men could stand in the bandstand in King's Square holding hands, declaring their love for one another. The men had a gathering of friends and family witnessing that love, and Hank found that both uplifting and heart-wrenching.

It was George in his dreams last night. First, they'd been sitting in the back row of the building he could see at the end of the block like they did when the Kent Theatre offered Saturday matinees. He and George would sit in the dark, sometimes daring to hold hands. A dark cloud of shame and pretense had been there for as long as Hank could remember and hadn't lifted even slightly until he walked up the steps of that SMT bus so long ago.

Regardless of what he'd lost, Hank knew in his heart he'd gained so much by leaving. If only Marvin had lived long enough for them to have stood together before witnesses, proclaiming their love. Last night's dream continued, and next it was he and George standing in the King's Square bandstand. The shorter man in the teal suit he'd seen yesterday was him in the dream. But was that beaming woman catching the bouquet his mother, or his daughter?

Hank turned the corner, knowing the futility of his imaginings. His life was coming to an end, and the love and acceptance he'd craved would never materialize. He must instead cling to the love he had known, and the angels he'd met along the way.

Maybe later he'd take a bus to Fernhill and stand awhile at Gramps's grave. Gramps, who started out as a stranger but ended up showing him more love, and caring about him more deeply, than his own father ever had.

Maybe he'd have lunch with Pearl or run into Bruce.

At the end of the day, he'd put his head down on Gloria's gaudy velvet couch and fall asleep in the twinkle of the Christmas tree lights on this, another Christmas Eve.

::

Jenny zipped up the garment bag holding Ryan's teal suit. He had looked so handsome and the day had been perfect. The wedding had been a surprise to her, but apparently the boys had been planning it for months. They had made the arrangements flexible so that whenever they came for the funeral, they could follow it up with a wedding. It had been a perfect mix of joy and sorrow.

The photographer took some lovely photos, and having them would make Ryan and Serge living so far away easier. She'd frame several and put them around her new apartment in the Wentworth Building. Move-in date was the first of January, something to look forward to. But for now, she would enjoy the time with Ryan and Serge, who were staying for Christmas and flying back to Toronto on Boxing Day.

Yesterday when they left King's Square and walked toward the car, she'd glanced over at two men sitting on a bench facing the Imperial. Caught up in the drama of Ryan's story about his grandmother taking him by the Imperial had her for a split second considering going over to them and asking if they knew a man named Hank. She'd quickly told herself how ridiculous it was to think two random men sitting in the square would know her father and be able to bring about a heartwarming reunion that would make up for sixty years of separation.

"We're going to Costco, Mom. Have you got a list?"

"A trip to Costco...not exactly the honeymoon of your dreams."

December 25, 2021

The doorbell woke Hank. The dark room was only illuminated by the twinkling Christmas tree lights and the stream of light coming from the streetlamp outside the window. As Hank reached to turn on the lamp, the doorbell rang again.

Hank opened the door a crack. A young man stood on the stoop, his arms holding a cardboard box and a Costco bag.

"Hank?"

"Yeah," Hank answered groggily.

"I'm Gloria's son, Kevin. She sent me in with your Christmas dinner."

Hank turned the hall light on and reached to take the Costco bag from the young man. "God love her. Come in. Sorry I was so long getting to the door. I was asleep."

"No problem," Kevin said, setting the box on the floor. "I won't bother taking my boots off to come in."

"What time of day is it?" Hank asked.

"It's almost seven o'clock," Kevin said. "I'd barely taken my last bite when Mom pushed me out the door."

Hank carried the bag into the kitchen and came back out for the box.

"There's a plate all dished up in that box," Kevin called into the kitchen. "All you have to do is nuke it. She sent in pickles, cranberry sauce, and three kinds of pie."

Hank returned to the hall. "She didn't have to send all that in. She already left me food in the fridge."

"That's Mom for you. She had herself all worked up, feeling so guilty you were alone with no Christmas dinner."

"Oh, my lord," Hank said. "There's nothing to feel guilty about. She has been a good friend and generous beyond words. She's letting me stay here until a room is available in a rooming house."

"Oh, she doesn't think that's good enough," Kevin said. "She has Dad convinced to let you move in for the winter."

"What do the rest of you think about her taking in an old homeless guy?"

"Mom's a pretty good judge of character, so if she wants to open her house to you, we're all right with that," Kevin answered. "I better get home. We're supposed to get a dumping of snow tonight. Enjoy your dinner, Hank. And it was nice to meet you."

"Nice to meet you too, Kevin. Thanks for bringing this in."

Hank shut the door and went into the kitchen to unpack everything. Through the small window he could see the snow had started falling in a flurry of small flakes, which meant a big snowfall. A snowfall to most people would seem a lovely end to Christmas day. But to the poor bastards sleeping outside in this city, a heavy snowfall was an additional hardship to be endured. Tears ran down Hank's cheeks as he pulled out the plate of food and put it in the microwave.

December 26, 2021

After clearing the front step and sidewalk outside the studio, Hank set the shovel back in the hallway. Stepping out again, he locked the front door. Knowing he had a warm, comfortable place to return to made strolling around on this sunny Boxing Day an inviting prospect. That hadn't been the case in the last two months when walking the uptown streets all day was a necessary part of surviving.

A man making his way through the narrow-plowed strip in the middle of the street stopped and walked the few steps back, stepping over the snowbank onto the small section of sidewalk Hank had just shovelled.

"Who are you?" the man asked.

"Pardon me?" Hank said.

"Well, I know you're not Mrs. Hamilton, and I'm quite sure you're not her husband either. She's closed today, I'm sure. Can I ask why you're coming out of her studio and why you have a key?"

"Can I ask who you are?" Hank replied.

"I'm Mrs. Hamilton's landlord. Again, I'll ask, who the hell are you? This is not a residential property, and if Mrs. Hamilton's studio is closed between Christmas and New Year's, I can't think of any reason you'd be coming out of it and I certainly don't know why you would have a key."

Hank bristled at the man's condescending tone. "I am a friend of Gloria's, and she asked me to check on things."

"What kind of things? There is a security system and I keep good tabs on my buildings. If she is having any maintenance issues, she needs to let me know."

"I will tell her you came by," Hank said, turning away dismissively.

"You can also tell her that if she has anyone living in her studio, she is breaking the terms of her lease," the man continued, raising his voice. "And I will be asking her for a list of anyone with a key for the front or back doors, and if you got a key without her knowledge, I will be reporting that to the police. You still haven't told me your name."

Hank turned around and glared at the man.

The man quickly pulled a cell phone from his pocket and snapped a picture. "A picture will be a better identifier than your name anyway. Unless of course you have a record for vagrancy or breaking and entering."

"Have a nice day, sir, and Merry Christmas," Hank said as he stepped over the snowbank and headed down the street.

::

Christmas dinner leftovers had never been a perk on Boxing Day when Miriam was growing up, mainly because there hadn't been a Christmas dinner to start with. The vast amount of food prepared at Romero House yesterday had fed close to five hundred people, but after cleanup, more turkeys were cooked to prepare for today's hot turkey sandwiches. The effort had been amazing to witness, and Miriam had caught herself feeling emotional more than once.

At first, she'd chalked it up to lack of sleep. But while dishing up the generous portions of Christmas dinner, she recalled the hunger and uncertainty she'd felt as a child. As Miriam closed each Styrofoam container lid, she imagined her ten-year-old self standing at the window to receive it.

On the drive home she'd let the tears fall, realizing that this had been the first Christmas for as long as she could remember that she'd felt any joy. So going back in again today seemed like a good thing to do. Maybe helping others brought more of a reward than she realized.

"Would you mind standing at the window and ladling up the gravy? I want these sandwiches to be as hot as possible. God, I wish we could invite the folks in, but I don't want to get shut down for not following COVID protocol."

Miriam tied her apron and fixed the hair net in place, surprised that for once she had no concern for her appearance. Maybe some of the generous, unselfish qualities of these amazing people were rubbing off on her.

::

Sitting in King's Square, Hank tried to settle his nerves from the altercation with Gloria's landlord. He'd considered turning around and going back to confront the man. On what grounds, though? Hank raged, thinking of the man's arrogance and dismissive tone. His threatening words and overall rudeness had shaken Hank, especially the words he'd shouted after him as he walked away.

"There are laws against squatting in this city. I just live across the street, and you can be sure I'll be keeping a close eye on the comings and goings in this building. If I see you around again, I'll be calling the police."

There was no way Hank was jeopardizing Gloria's tenancy. She'd worked hard to set up her studio and establish her location. Getting her evicted would not be the way to repay the generosity she'd shown him. He obviously could not return at least until she was open again for business. Surely her landlord couldn't dictate who she let in during business hours.

He could manage a couple of nights in the shelter. People were overly generous this time of year, and several other locations had been opened to accommodate the homeless. He could probably get some toiletries there. Luckily, he'd dressed warmly before leaving. Gloria would be back in her studio the day after tomorrow, and they would figure something out then. Maybe as Kevin said, Ted had given in and Hank could stay in Gloria's house for the winter. If he had to, he could probably get into the Imperial in the next couple of days and get his things. Even if Liam wasn't working, others there knew him now and would let him get the shopping cart Liam had stuck in the storeroom by the service entrance.

He had been looking forward to the portion of Christmas dinner he'd saved and the last piece of pie, but instead of chancing it, he'd walk to Romero House and see what was on the menu for lunch. "Every cloud has a silver lining," Gran always said.

::

Miriam decided to pass out five more meals before taking a bathroom and smoke break. The lines had been long and steady. It was heartbreaking to think that so many people relied on this place, and that after feeding hundreds of people today, it needed to be done all over again tomorrow. The bright and sparkling sun on the fresh snow gave a positive feel to the day but did nothing to change the reality that many of these people had slept outside last night in the worst of the storm.

Miriam ladled on the gravy and closed the lid of another container. Looking out the window she noticed the man she'd seen a few times at Gloria Hamilton's studio. Hank, she'd called him, and Miriam had texted Jenny about him. As far as she knew, Jenny hadn't found him yet to verify if he might be her father. With her mother's passing and Ryan's wedding, Jenny had had other concerns.

"I'm going to take a quick break," Miriam said. "Marie, can you do the gravy until I get back?"

Miriam considered her approach. The man was almost to the window, and bothering him when he was probably eager to get his meal seemed wrong. Interrupting him after he got it and preventing him from eating it while it was hot seemed even worse. If she went back to her station, chances are he'd be long gone before she got another chance to talk to him. And she couldn't very well just lean out the window and blurt out her question.

Miriam opened the drop-off door and walked outside. There were still several others in front of Hank.

"Hank, can I talk to you for minute? I know you don't want to lose your place, but I can go in and get you a meal when we've finished talking."

Miriam could see that Hank looked a bit confused, but he stepped out of line and walked toward her.

"You're not selling this building too, are ya?"

"No, I'm not," Miriam laughed. "I'm volunteering, which seems a stretch even to me. Want to sit in my car for a minute while we talk? I promise I'll get you a meal as soon as we're finished."

Miriam led Hank to her parked SUV down the street. He slid into the passenger seat as she got in the driver's side.

"Okay, I'll get right to the point," Miriam said. "My friend Jenny's father's name was Hank. He left Saint John in the early sixties, I think. Her mother's name was Tanya. Are you her father?"

Miriam looked over, waiting for Hank to respond, feeling discomfort with the silence. What had made her think she'd swoop in and find Jenny's missing father?

Miriam saw that Hank was unzipping the leather pouch at his waist and pulling out a photograph.

"Jennifer Dawn, born the second of January, 1959. That makes her almost sixty-three years old by my calculations," Hank said, passing the photograph to Miriam.

"Oh my God," Miriam said. "She will be so happy to have found you."

"Really? I can't imagine why."

"Is it okay if I text her and tell her I've been talking to you?"

"I have tried to find her over the years," Hank said, emotion rising in his voice. "Can you tell her that? Things just never seemed to fall into place."

"I can do even better than that, Hank," Miriam said. "I know she wants to connect with you. We can set something up, maybe someplace she could meet you. I'm sure she'd come right away. I can text her and see if she replies."

"Yeah, I guess you could do that. Unfortunately, I don't have anywhere that I can invite her in to meet me, but maybe if she meets me in King's Square we could walk down to Tim Horton's and have a coffee."

"Okay. I'm going to text her right away. Hopefully she'll answer me right back and we can make a plan. I'll run in and get your meal, then I've got to get back to my station. I'm the gravy lady."

::

Hank sat on the steps of the nearby call centre to eat his not-so-hot turkey sandwich. He'd waited a few minutes after she brought out his meal, but Miriam Ross hadn't come back out with a message from Jennifer. A reunion was too good to be true anyway. Why would anyone put themselves through the trouble of trudging through the snow in King's Square to meet up with some homeless guy claiming to be their father? His daughter probably had better things to do on Boxing Day.

::

Jenny hated goodbyes and always insisted on pulling up to the Departures door and dropping Ryan off. After he got his luggage, she'd allow a quick kiss on the cheek through the driver's window before pulling away. This time had been no easier, especially when Serge insisted she get out to give him a hug.

"I told him you don't do goodbyes, Mom, but he's not giving up," Ryan said. "You may as well just get out and hug him."

"Are you sure you're not coming in to see us off, at least until we get through security?" Serge asked.

"Now you're really pushing it," Jenny said. "Just because you're my son-in-law now doesn't mean you get to change my goodbye routine. Now get going, the two of you, before you make me cry."

Before driving away, Jenny quickly checked her phone. Miriam had sent a text hours ago. She'd missed it in all the chaos of getting the boys to the airport for their flight.

Second day at Romero House and I found your dad. He wants to meet you in King's Square this afternoon.

Jenny swiped at her face. If she gave in to this, all the emotion built up in the last few weeks would cascade to the surface, and she wasn't sure she could stop it. She hadn't even cried at the funeral, telling herself it was relief she felt, not sadness. She was very emotional witnessing Ryan and Serge say their vows, but cried no tears, unwilling to let the event overwhelm her. Now she was finally getting to meet her father and maybe have a little bit of time to catch up on what she'd missed out on her whole life. This might be what broke the dam.

No, she would not cry yet. She would drive to King's Square and hopefully he would still be there. This time, unlike the day of Ryan's wedding, she really would take the risk and walk up to as many men as she needed to till she found the right one: her father.

::

The snow was deep in the square, as crews had not been out to clear the walkways. Hank could have gone to the nearest bench, or even walked along the street until reaching what he considered to be his bench. Instead, he had trudged through the snow all the way across the square to sit facing the Imperial Theatre. Looking down King, Hank could see the setting sun. Only a few more minutes of daylight left, but the day felt warmer now that the wind had died down. The snow glistened as the Christmas lights shone brightly. Hank swivelled his head, noting that he was the only person in the square. Jennifer would have no confusion finding him if she came. There was no guarantee she'd even read the text Miriam had sent her.

Hank turned back and stared at the doors of the Imperial. He thought back to the June morning he'd gone into that building to join Tanya's family at Sunday service. The nervousness he'd felt that day was different from what he was feeling right now, but both held a mix of fear, doubt, uncertainty, and shame. How would he explain to his daughter that the choices he made had never been because he didn't love her?

::

As Jenny drove across the causeway, her mind sifted through thoughts of what she would say if he was there. Any anger she'd felt had long dispersed, and too many years had gone by to let resentment and blame cloud this reunion. She just wanted to look in her father's eyes, the eyes her grandmother always said were the image of her own; she wanted to see a flicker of the love she'd always believed he had for her, and tell him how much she loved him.

Turning on to Crown Street, she saw a text notification on the screen. She pushed *Read* to hear the robotic delivery of Ryan's text.

Our flight's been cancelled and rescheduled for tomorrow. Can you come back to the airport and get us?

Jenny hit the automatic *yes* reply. She would go to the airport and pick up Ryan and Serge and come right back, bringing them with her. Ryan would meet his grandfather at the same time she reconnected with her father.

:::

Hank realized as six bells rang out from the church across the street that he'd been sitting waiting for almost four hours. He had gotten up and walked around a bit to keep the cold at bay, but if he stayed much longer it might be a frozen corpse his daughter discovered when or if she arrived. Hank pondered his options. He could go back to Gloria's and sneak in the back door. He'd leave footprints in the snow, but surely Gloria's landlord's surveillance did not include hourly checks around the entire building. Once inside he could leave the lights off and possibly stay undetected until morning, then sneak out the back door again. He wasn't sure, though, if his key would work in the back door. If he wanted a spot at any of the shelters, he'd best get to one soon; they filled up quickly this time of day. He might even get there in time for supper. He could go without a meal, but wouldn't refuse one.

Either way, waiting any longer seemed pointless. His daughter probably wouldn't be too keen to tramp through King's Square at this time of day, and Tim Horton's normally closed at seven o'clock and maybe earlier on a holiday. He had to be realistic and let go of the fantasy that today was the day he would get to see Jennifer. Hank stood up and started walking. He'd try Stone Church first, and if they were full, he'd try Outflow.

:::

Ruth King hung up the phone and slumped into the nearby chair. She'd always accused her mother of spoiling her Boxing Day birthday, but Pearl dying on it was a new low. This time of year was hard enough, Christmas never having been Pearl's soberest time, and throwing her only daughter's birthday into the mix just another reason to drink herself into oblivion. Just once it would have been nice if her mother kept back one of the few presents she'd managed to buy for Christmas and at least acknowledged her daughter's birthday.

The acknowledgment usually didn't come until a few days after and the greeting was always the same. *You were supposed to be born in January. Ruined my Christmas that year.* "You've got me beat on that count, Mother. You ruined all my Christmases, and my birthdays."

::

Hank sat down at the long table after setting his tray down. The turkey dinner on the plate did not look as appetizing as Gloria's, but Hank wasn't one to find fault with a free hot meal. The makeshift dining hall was decorated with some Christmas lights and a few strands of garland. Marvin had loved the garland and anything glittery, and for their first Christmas in the house he'd purchased an aluminum artificial tree at Macy's. Marvin took great pains in decorating it, hanging each strand of tinsel separately and carefully placing the array of colourful glass ornaments.

When packing up the house, Hank had put the tree and the boxes of decorations out on the curb with a sign saying *Free.* After deciding to go back to Saint John he'd sold most of the household items, but somehow it seemed right to offer the tree for free to some passersby in hopes that maybe it would bring someone else as much joy as it had given Marvin.

"Lights out at ten o'clock. Breakfast will be served starting at six-thirty."

Hank always chuckled at that announcement whenever he stayed in a shelter. Grown men put to bed at ten o'clock seemed a bit condescending. But most guys were happy to settle down for the night as soon as they arrived, after being in the elements all day and having many nights when sleep was erratic and unpredictable. Shelters enforced an early curfew hoping to discourage rowdiness, along with the hopes of providing several hours of sleep before folks started moving around in the morning.

December 27, 2021

*L*ooking at the clock on the bedside table, Liam saw it was 3:15. Sadie had been waking up the last few nights, and it was his turn to go to her. It was probably the excitement of Christmas and change in routine that were disrupting her sleep patterns. Rocking her in her darkened bedroom and playing some music usually worked to get her back to sleep. Before lifting Sadie from her crib, Liam typed *The Mamas & the Papas* into his phone and selected Sadie's favourite song, "California Dreamin'".

As Liam was placing a sleeping Sadie back in her bed, he felt a twinge of panic and realized his thoughts were of Hank. He'd only seen Hank a couple of times since he'd helped unload Alan Doyle's equipment. His shopping cart was still in the storeroom, and Liam felt relieved he hadn't come back for it; that meant he hadn't had to set up another encampment. As far as he knew, Hank was sleeping at a friend's place until he could get into the rooming house around the corner from the Imperial.

By the time Liam got back into his own bed, he'd decided he'd go to Saint John in the morning and see if he could find Hank just to make sure he was okay. He didn't have to work until after New Year's, but he wasn't willing to wait that long. He'd take him to breakfast and give him the little gift he'd bought him.

::

Hank woke with a start to the yelling and loud protests just a few cots away from his.

"Get away from me, you sick faggot."

Hank sat up. That vile word still brought instant nausea and caused his pulse to quicken. The lights snapped on as three men rushed into the room.

"I'll cut your fuckin pecker off."

Hank saw the knife as the kid hollering flipped open the blade. Blood spurted as the older guy grabbed his thigh.

One of the men who'd entered the room picked up a chair and, using it as a shield, moved slowly toward the attacker. "Call 911, Tony."

Tony punched numbers into his phone and motioned to the third man.

"Everybody clear out," the third guy hollered. "Grab your stuff and get outside. We don't want anyone else getting hurt."

Hank was one of the first out the door. The cold air hit him, ending any grogginess or confusion he'd felt being woken up so abruptly. The sound of sirens getting closer was enough to scatter the thirty or so men gathered on the sidewalk. Police presence did not mean safety and comfort to most of them.

Hank put the sleeping bag around his shoulders and started walking away. The chances of getting back inside tonight were slim. He could see the sun just peeking up on the horizon. He'd head to King's Square and lie down on his bench for an hour or so.

::

Ryan shook his mother gently. "I just got a text, Mom. We've got an early flight. That will get us home by nine. We can take a cab if you don't want to take us to the airport."

"Don't be ridiculous. Of course I'll take you. Just give me a minute."

"You don't have to rush. I'm sure if we're there by five it will be fine."

"I'm coming in this time and waiting until you get on the plane."

"Oh, wow. What have you done with my mother."

::

King's Square had an eerie beauty as Hank made his way through. The snow was more tramped down than yesterday, but again he found himself the only occupant. He wondered where the other men leaving the shelter had gone for refuge but found himself glad it hadn't been here. This square held such memory and attachment for him.

Sitting down, he unzipped his leather pouch and pulled out his treasured photographs. How lucky he was to have them, even though looking at them sometimes brought such sadness. He held the little pile to his heart before viewing them one by one and breathing them in.

The top one was an older black-and-white photo, taken on the sidewalk in front of the house on Adelaide. George was standing tall astride his new Western Flyer bicycle. It had been red and had a parcel carrier on the back. Hank could hardly keep up with him on his old rickety CCM.

The second was a square photo, edged with a white border that looked as if it had been trimmed with his Gran's pinking shears. A coloured photograph, the shades muted by time. Jennifer was wearing a pink nightie and his shirt was a brown plaid. He'd been so young to be thrust into fatherhood, but he recalled the joy he'd felt when the nurse put his baby into his arms.

Next a wrinkled school picture: 1970, grade six. Jennifer had been eleven years old, and for some reason this was the only one of the school pictures his mother had sent him over the years that he still had. There had been something about her eyes and her smile that had drawn him to that photograph more powerfully than the others, and he'd always kept it in his wallet. Looking at it now, he realized just how much the face he saw resembled his own.

A Polaroid next, of Jennifer holding Ryan, and it always brought a tear to his eye. Of all the sacrifices he'd made, perhaps not knowing his grandson was the costliest. That had been his fantasy yesterday as he sat waiting for Jennifer. Maybe, just maybe, she'd have Ryan with her, and he could put his arms around the boy, now a man, and tell him how much he loved him and how deeply he regretted not being a part of his growing-up years.

Hank slipped the photographs back into his pouch without looking at the last one. He could not bear the sorrow of it. It had been such a hopeful time, and he remembered the day it was taken as if it was yesterday. The sun had been so strong, the smell of the spring blossoms so fragrant. Hank's hair was a very manageable James Dean style while Marvin, embracing the hippy life, let his own hair flow, uncovered. A breeze had been blowing and Marvin kept trying to put his hair back in place.

Roberto had taken the picture with his new Canon and kept chastising Hank for not being more demonstrative with his affection as he posed them. Hank had at the last minute leaned in to kiss Marvin's cheek, and Roberto had snapped the picture.

Hank took the photo out. He rolled the sleeping bag up to make a pillow and lay down on the bench, clutching the photo to his chest for a few seconds before slipping it back into the leather pouch. A heavy weariness came over him and he closed his eyes. Music filled the silence and he was sitting at the soundboard. Through the glass he could see Denny, Michelle, Cass, and John, each moving perfectly in synch with the melody, singing about being safe and warm.

::

Gloria had set the alarm, determined to put Hank's room in order before ten. She'd stripped the bed yesterday and the clean bedding sat in the laundry basket at the foot of the bed. First she would empty the dresser drawers, then the closet. Most of the contents could be donated, and some things thrown away. Why she'd kept the clutter of this room she didn't know, but she would have it emptied out completely so Hank would have plenty of space for his own things.

One thing she was happy to leave in the room was Kevin's old stereo. She couldn't believe the luck she'd had getting Gordie Tufts to round up some of the albums with Hank's name in the credits. She'd wrapped the seven albums and had almost sent them in with Kevin on Christmas day but wanted to be there when Hank opened them. Later this morning, she would drive in and give him his gift. Hopefully she would be able to convince him to come home with her and live with them at least for the winter months.

Gloria took the painting off the wall. It had been one of her early ones, and looking at it she realized how far her work had come. She would find another place in the house to hang it. This spot would hold a painting by another artist.

Gloria picked up the print and positioned it on the empty nail. She had touched it up just a little bit, but the painting was Hank's. The fishing boat seemed to be moving in tumultuous waves. The fog was heavy and the darkening sky foreboding.

"Does it make you sad to look at this?" she'd asked Hank the day he finished the painting, and he told her of George's drowning.

"No. I was sad for a very long time, and then one day it occurred to me that just as I had made a choice to leave the day I caught a bus out of Saint John, George made a choice too. He loved the sea, and if he jumped from that boat on purpose as they say he did, then I choose to believe he made the choice that was right for him."

::

Liam pulled in to the employee parking behind the theatre and quickly got out of his car. All the way in on the highway he'd felt an inexplicable sense of urgency. As he walked up Charlotte toward the square, a flustered woman nearly ran into him.

"I think there's a dead guy on a bench in the square," the woman said. "I called 911."

Liam ran to the corner and bolted across the street. "Hank!" he shouted.

Dropping to his knees, Liam shook Hank gently. Hank's eyes were closed, but leaning in, Liam felt the warmth of his friend's shallow breath. He unzipped Hank's hood and placed two fingers under his chin, finding a faint pulse. The strobing lights of an ambulance came into sight.

"Hank. It's me. It's Liam. You're okay, Hank. You're okay."

Hank's head moved slightly.

Liam felt a gripping fear that Hank would be dead before the ambulance attendants got around the square and parked.

::

Jenny had hardly managed to drive, her vision impaired by the steady stream of tears she'd been wiping the whole way from the airport. She parked on Wentworth, looking up at the window that would soon be hers. Last night she'd taken out the Mama & the Papas album *If You Can Believe Your Eyes and Ears*. She'd loved the cover art when she bought it and still got a kick out of seeing the four singers squeezed into the bathtub. Being someone who liked a bath rather than a shower, she'd made sure her new apartment had a nice, big bathtub.

Jenny was looking forward to a new start in that fifth-floor apartment. Her focus went from the window to the sculpture and bench created using stone from the old Gothic Arches. It was a somewhat underwhelming memorial to the grand structure that had once stood on this site.

She'd read about the groundbreaking union that had taken place there in 1998 and kept thinking about how different Ryan's life might be if men like Carl Trickey and Jim Crooks hadn't courageously paved the way. Her own father growing up gay in the 1950s had had very few choices, and she was no longer resentful of him making the choice to leave.

Jenny started up her car again and drove around the corner, parking on Princess. Today was the day she would find him. It had been disappointing yesterday, finding nobody waiting in King's Square. She hadn't even told Ryan why she had driven uptown instead of going right home.

Jenny got out, pulling on her toque and mittens. She crossed the street and walked along the snow-packed sidewalk past the tall Irving building. Rounding the corner, she saw emergency vehicles. An ambulance was pulling away with its lights flashing. A police car was parked in front of the Imperial and two officers were talking to a man. Getting closer she overheard the conversation.

"No, I'm not related. But he's not just some homeless guy. He's my friend."

"You know his name, then?"

"Yes, I know his name. His name is Hank Lowman. Hank Lowman. You should google him!"

Jenny stopped, letting the man's words sink in. Was her father in that ambulance? The lights had been flashing. Did they turn the lights on if the patient was dead? A panic rose in Jenny's throat and she rushed up to the officers.

"I'm Hank Lowman's daughter," Jenny said.

Liam turned to her. "Jennifer?"

"Is he dead?" Jenny stammered.

"No," Liam answered emphatically. "His vitals are good. They have him on oxygen and a heart monitor. He's a strong guy, your dad. I'm going right to the hospital. You can come with me if you want."

"Who are you?" Jenny asked.

"Oh right. Sorry. My name's Liam. I am a friend of Hank's."

::

Ruth King walked up the stairway to Pearl's door. She inserted the key and turned the knob. Neither Kenny nor David had been willing to tackle this with her, so cleaning out her mother's apartment was something she would have to do alone. The landlord had been kind but insisted it be done today so he could have the apartment cleaned and ready for a new tenant by January 2. How long would it take to pack up or dispose of her mother's life?

Driving along Charlotte, she'd seen a police car and an ambulance parked in front of the Imperial. They seemed to be removing someone from a bench. At least that wasn't where her mother had died. But how terrible was it that she hadn't even known where her mother lived? How had so much time gone by and she'd never made the effort to reach out to her mother? She'd long since forgiven her, but for some reason hadn't been able to tell her that.

::

Miriam turned the light on in the dim office. No other agents were working today, but she'd come in to get the file for a property that seemed to be very close to closing. She'd already shown the home to the clients three times, but they'd asked for one more viewing before making up their minds.

It was a beautiful property, and when listing it Miriam had been astonished by its transformation. She could hardly imagine it as it had been. What was now a one family dwelling, totally refurbished and elegant, had been three flats, the middle floor being the shabby one she'd grown up in. Nothing about the exterior or the interior resembled the building she remembered. but even seeing the address on the paperwork caused heart palpitations. She would be glad to close this deal and let the property, and the memories of living there, go. Maybe by doing that she could also let go of the memories of living there.

On her way in she'd noticed Jenny's orange RAV parked on Princess and wondered what she was doing uptown this early. Miriam was anxious to hear how the reunion with Hank had gone. She'd text her later and maybe they could meet somewhere for lunch.

::

Jenny took the cup of vending machine coffee Liam passed her, concentrating all her attention on the rising steam and aroma, as if it were a lifeline of some kind. The drive to the hospital had been surreal, and neither she nor Liam had spoken on the way over. Liam walked back over with his own coffee and sat beside her in the empty ER waiting room.

"How long have you known my dad?" Jenny asked.

"I only met him in November. But I see him most every day I'm at work. I work at the Imperial."

"You knew my name. Did he talk about me?"

Liam picked up the leather pouch from the chair beside him. He'd removed it from under Hank's parka before the paramedics had lifted the stretcher into the back of the ambulance.

"Hank is never without this," Liam said passing the pouch to Jenny. "He says it holds all his treasures."

Jenny set her coffee cup down and unzipped the pouch. The first thing she pulled out was a postcard-sized painting. On the back it said Tin Can Beach.

"My mother took me there once," Jenny said as she set the postcard down on the table. "She told me my great-grandmother used to live in one of the houses we could see across the water."

"The artist is a good friend of your dad's. He's been staying in her studio for the last week or so. I'm not sure why he was in the square this morning."

"Has he been living on the street?" Jenny asked.

"The rooming house he lived in for a few years sold in October and he was evicted. He constructed a shelter on the bank of the causeway and was there for a while but the city destroyed it. His artist friend has a studio on Germain and she's been letting him stay there. He's on a waiting list to get into Lantern House on Princess."

"My friend served him at Romero House yesterday. We were supposed to meet in King's Square but I got waylaid. When I showed up later, he wasn't there. Maybe he came back this morning in case I came by."

"Either way, Jennifer, you can't feel guilty."

"I started one other day to try to find him. Got called away that day too."

"I know he tried to find you several times over the years. Seems so unfair the way things worked out. But you need to know how much he loves you. Look and see what else he carries in that pouch."

Jenny pulled out the pictures. "This was my grade six picture. I hated that haircut. This baby is my son, the other baby is me. Do you know who that man is? I assume the one with the short hair is my father."

"His name was Marvin. The photograph was taken in San Francisco. He was your father's partner."

"I've always hated the term 'partner' and hate 'life partner' even more," Jenny said. "I've used it sometimes, though, when I told people about Serge. I'm glad I can say Ryan's husband now, but I know my dad wasn't given that option, not legally anyway. Is Marvin still alive?"

"No, he died before your dad came back to Saint John. He didn't tell me much, but I know he died from injuries he suffered after a brutal attack."

Jenny placed all the photographs back in the pouch and fastened it around her waist.

"Thank you for this, Liam."

"Those photographs are his most important possessions."

Jenny glanced at her phone surprised by the time. Ryan and Serge would be home by now, but she would wait until she knew more about her father's condition before calling them.

"Your dad has other friends besides me and the artist," Liam said. "He's been getting close to a woman named Pearl and a guy named Bruce who works for the city."

Both Liam and Jenny focused on their coffee for the next few minutes. A few people came into Emerg, but still no one had come to tell them they could go in.

"Your dad is a good guy," Liam said as he stood to put his cup in the garbage. "He hasn't had it easy, but he doesn't complain much. He's taught me a thing or two."

"You told the paramedic to google him. Was that because of the work he did in the recording industry?"

"Yes. He was a big deal in his day. I'm in awe at what he accomplished. He has had quite a life, you know. Not an easy one, but one I certainly admire."

"Could you maybe help me find his other friends?" Jenny asked.

"Yeah, for sure," Liam said. "When I drive you back, we could go to Gloria's art studio. Maybe she'll be there. She'll be thrilled to meet you."

Jenny took a tissue from her coat pocket and wiped the tears from her cheeks.

"I'll go ask the woman at the desk if she can tell us anything yet," Liam said.

::

Ryan pulled the large suitcase through the door of the apartment. Looking around, it was evident how quickly they had left after getting the call the day Nan died. Serge would soon have things in order and no doubt, despite their early morning and the exhaustion of the last few weeks, assign him several cleaning duties as well. Possibly there was an option that might distract Serge from full-out housecleaning.

"Thought we might just relax and watch a movie," Ryan said as Serge hung his coat in the hall closet.

"A movie? We've got too much to do to watch a movie. We need to unpack, and this place is a mess."

Knowing Serge's obsession with and his adoration for Sean Penn, Ryan continued. "I downloaded one I think you'd drop everything to watch, and it's possibly one of Sean's best performances aside from your beloved *I Am Sam*."

Serge came into the living room and sat on the edge of the couch.

"What about *Mystic River* or *Dead Man Walking*?"

"I downloaded *Milk*. I think it's a perfect movie for us to curl up and watch our first morning back home as a married couple. God, I had no idea until I googled the guy just what an impact he had."

"Sean Penn plays Harvey Milk? How did I miss that?"

"Too busy fighting our own fight, I guess. Mom says my grandfather lived in San Francisco in the sixties and seventies. He might have even known Harvey Milk."

"Make some popcorn then, sweetie. You sold me at Sean Penn. But if you fall asleep, I'm waking you up. And as soon as the movie is over, we're slopping out this place. I cannot live in such squalor."

::

Jenny and Liam both stood and nodded as a nurse approached, inquiring if they were Hank Lowman's family.

"You go in first, Jenny," Liam said.

"I'd like you to come in with me," Jenny said. "He'll have no idea who I am, but he'll know you. That's if he's conscious."

"He is awake," the nurse said. "He still has the oxygen mask on, so he hasn't spoken."

Jenny felt a wave of nausea as the nurse pulled back the curtain. She stumbled a bit and Liam reached for her arm. The man in the bed looked so small and vulnerable. Tubes ran from the IV stand and the oxygen tank emitted an eerie whirr. Wispy white hair covered the old man's head and white whiskers covered his face and his eyes were barely open.

"Your kids are here, Mr. Lowman," the nurse said with exaggerated enthusiasm.

::

Gloria knocked on the door again before putting the key in the lock. All the way in she'd hardly been able to contain her excitement. It felt so good filling Hank's dresser with the assortment of socks, T-shirts, and underwear she'd bought him. She'd removed all the tags first, laying everything out on the bed.

"How do you know if he prefers boxers or briefs?" Ted asked jokingly.

"I don't know," Gloria answered. "That's why I bought ten of each."

"Dear God, woman. This guy's going to have more clothes than I ever thought of having."

"That's not true. I wanted to make sure he had lots of choice. He's hardly had a change of clothes these last few months. I bought him a new winter coat too. I hope he doesn't take offence to that."

Ted picked up the coat and pretended to put it on. "I'll take it if he doesn't want it. In case you haven't noticed, I've been wearing the same one forever."

"Oh, I know, you're so hard done by," Gloria said. "After I'm done here, I'm heading into the city. My plan is to bring Hank home today. Did you want to come in with me?"

"No. You go do your good Samaritan thing and I'll keep the furnace going and make my famous turkey pot pie for supper. And just so you know, I think you're pretty amazing. That old guy is lucky to have met you."

Walking into the hallway, Gloria called out Hank's name but got no answer. Looking in to the studio, she noticed the blankets folded neatly at the end of the couch. In the fridge she saw a cellophane-wrapped plate with part of the supper she'd sent in Christmas night and one piece of pie. Apparently, Hank was rationing the food somewhat, which she supposed made sense; he didn't know she was coming in today.

Walking back into the studio, Gloria decided she would paint awhile, hoping Hank would come back soon. That seemed a better plan than going out to try to find him.

::

Jenny walked around the corner, trying to find a spot away from the hustle and chaos of the emergency room. Pulling out her cell phone, she called Ryan's number, hoping she'd be able to speak when he answered. It had been overwhelming to hear the doctor's explanation of her father's condition and the miracle of his survival. Had Liam been a few minutes later, he probably would have found Hank dead. And if Liam had stayed home this morning, she might have found her father minutes after he'd taken his last breath.

Those facts alone were emotional blows, but she'd been unprepared for what came next.

"Hank. Jennifer is here," Liam said coming close to the bed and touching Hank's shoulder.

Hank had turned his head toward her, his eyes filling with tears. She'd clasped his hand and he in turn had squeezed hers. The silent and emotional reunion, requiring no words or fanfare, had been as amazing as anything she'd imagined.

"I found your grandfather," Jenny blurted out, knowing how ridiculous that announcement would seem to Ryan. "He was in the square the day of your wedding."

"Mom?" Ryan said as he waited for his mother's sobbing to subside.

"I saw him the day of your wedding. I almost went up to him."

"Mom, calm down and tell me what's happening."

After composing herself, Jenny began by telling Ryan that she'd been looking for his grandfather for a few weeks since realizing he was still alive and likely living in Saint John. She explained how Miriam had texted her on Boxing Day but she'd missed him, returned to King's Square this morning, and what she had found upon arriving.

"He has congestive heart disease, and this morning he suffered a pulmonary edema."

"Mom, you know I'm a teacher, not a doctor, right?" Ryan said.

"I know it's a lot to take in. But the main thing is, we still have him. He knew me, Ryan. He looked right at me and he knew me. I wonder if I'd gone up to him on the day of your wedding if he would have known me. Why didn't I go up to him that day? You could have met your grandfather."

"Mom, are you all right? Do you want me to book a flight?"

"No, don't be silly, Ryan. I am fine. He is going to be in the hospital for a few days. They have to get his heart rate steadied and his oxygen levels up. He's a bit dehydrated and undernourished. He's been living on the street for almost two months. I will call you when I get home and tell you more. I know I'm a bit flustered, but we'll figure it out."

"You should call someone, Mom. Miriam maybe. Get her to come meet you. You shouldn't be alone."

"I'm not alone. Your grandfather's friend Liam is with me."

"Okay, Mom. Just take it easy and you'll be fine. I love you. And tell my grandfather I love him."

Jenny ended the call. She texted Miriam a quick message. *I found my dad. Text me.*

::

Bruce poured the water into the coffee maker. It was almost noon. He'd woken up earlier around five, from a dream in which he and Hank were sitting front row at a Bob Dylan concert. Weirdly, Hank was a young man, whereas he was his current age. Bob Dylan was announcing that Hank Lowman was in the front row. The crowd cheered as Hank stood to be acknowledged.

Bruce had woken from the dream sobbing. He'd gotten out of bed and put the *Blood on the Tracks* album on the turntable, going directly to "Meet me in the Morning." After listening to it the second time, Bruce got back into bed, a peace invading the overwhelming sadness the dream and song had left him with.

He'd fill a thermos, grab two mugs, and go try to find Hank. If he wasn't in the square, he'd go to where Hank was staying on Germain. Hank would get a real kick out of the dream. And of course, Hank would remind him that he'd been the one to convince him not to sell his Bob Dylan albums.

::

Gloria heard the bell and rushed to the door.

"Did you lose your key, Hank?" Gloria called out before opening the door and realizing it wasn't Hank standing on her stoop.

"Are you Gloria?" Bruce Smith asked. "I'm Hank's friend, Bruce."

"Is he all right?" Gloria asked, realizing she'd been tense with worry.

"He's not here?" Bruce asked.

"No, I got here a while ago expecting he'd be here, but he must have stepped out for a bit. You're the guy who works for the city, right?"

"That's me."

"Come in," Gloria said opening the door wider. "I'm sure Hank will show up soon. I'll put the kettle on."

::

Miriam entered the hospital parking lot feeling a jolt of dread similar to the feeling she had every time she'd come to see her mother. And now Jenny was back here again with the father she'd missed out on having her whole life. From the texts back and forth, Miriam had only understood a bit of what had transpired, and quickly told Jenny she would come and meet her at their old stomping ground.

Walking up the stairs to Tim Horton's, Miriam could see Jenny sitting in the far corner. Miriam quickly bought herself a coffee and sat down.

"The square was empty when I went yesterday," Jenny blurted out as soon as Miriam sat down. "I went back early this morning, and I keep thinking it was my fault he was there in the cold."

"None of this is your fault," Miriam said firmly. "You are just over-whelmed by it all. He's still alive and that's the main thing."

"I'm going to ask him to move in with me at Wentworth Place," Jenny said.

"Now, slow down. I understand that you are happy to have your father back in your life, but you don't know anything about him. You haven't

SUSAN WHITE

even been able to talk to him yet. Some tears and a hand clasp don't mean you move him in and take care of him. Do you even know how sick he is?"

"We've all those years to make up for. He's not going back on the street, Miriam. He deserves to have his family in his last days."

"Okay, I understand how you are feeling, but don't do anything drastic," Miriam said. "Keep packing and preparing for your move, but don't commit to anything just yet. I will be your hardhearted voice of reason."

"Okay. I hear you. Ryan has another week off after New Year's, so I'm going to ask him to come help me move and figure out the best plan for Dad."

"Well, that makes me feel better," Miriam said. "Ryan will talk some sense into you." She took a swig of her coffee and reached over to take a Timbit. "Is this all you've eaten? And you must be exhausted. Is there anything you want me to do for you?"

"Liam said Dad was staying at a friend's place, an artist on Germain," Jenny said. "Liam was going to take me there, but I told him you were coming and you'd take me to get my car. I told him to go home."

"And I'm telling you to go home," Miriam said, standing up. "Her name is Gloria. I will stop in and tell her about Hank after I drop you off to get your car.

Jenny pulled her coat on and picked up her garbage. She fell into step with Miriam, realizing just how tired she was.

December 28, 2021

*G*loria stopped outside Hank's hospital room to put on the paper gown and face mask required to enter. She had gone to the hospital right after Miriam Ross had come to tell her about Hank but she hadn't been allowed to see him in Emerg. Jenny had called her this morning telling her Hank had been moved to a room and could have visitors provided they passed a COVID test and took the necessary precautions.

Hank opened his eyes as Gloria entered the room.

"Dorothy?" Hank asked.

"No, it's Gloria."

"Oh, sorry," Hank said. "I've been thinking so much about my friend Dorothy. I was sure I heard her voice last night just as I was going to sleep. I've been hearing a jumble of voices, truth be told. Must be the medication they have me on."

"You gave us a scare, Hank. Has Bruce been in yet?"

"He was in just a while ago. Liam and Amanda were in earlier too. I'm getting lots of visitors. And Jennifer's bringing Ryan to meet me tomorrow. Who would have thought an old guy like me would be so popular?"

"That daughter of yours is lovely. She's some happy you're all right, I can tell you."

"I still can't believe the good Lord let me live long enough to see her again. I remember lying down on that bench, Gloria. I was cold and feeling so tired. I was just so tired. I felt so weak and so alone but I wasn't afraid. I felt like I was on my way to Marvin, to George, to Dorothy and Gramps and to Mama Cass. It wasn't my time, I guess."

Gloria leaned in and touched Hank's cheek.

"No, it was not your time, and we are going to make sure you are not alone when that time does come."

"God love Gloria. That's what Jennifer keeps saying. I am one lucky old man."

January 5, 2022

H ank got slowly out of the passenger side of Jenny's RAV, which was parked behind the large moving van. Jenny and Ryan had gone up to check on the progress being made unloading the furniture and boxes. Jenny suggested he stay in the car. They wouldn't be long; they were meeting Gloria and Bruce at Britt's for lunch in half an hour. Jenny had even offered to leave the motor running, but Hank assured her he would be warm enough.

"I've got this fancy new coat Gloria bought for me and the sun is shining. I'll be fine," Hank said.

Hank looked up, counting to the fifth floor where Jenny's apartment was. He turned to take in the surrounding buildings, unchanged and familiar, and felt an overwhelming sadness for the grand structure that once stood in the place of this new one. Wentworth Place. He took some steps, taking in the stone sculpture, benches, and table in front of the building. He squeezed onto one of the benches at the square, marble table.

In his dream last night, Dorothy had driven up to the west side apartment. It was a different car she was driving, but her rainbow-coloured hair and bright attire were exactly as Hank remembered them.

"You take family where you can find it, Hank. Sometimes it's flesh and blood and sometimes it's a chance meeting or someone you sit beside in church when all the other seats are taken. Sometimes family is heartbreaking. We fall short and make mistakes. Family sometimes lets us down. But friends can step up and fill our empty places, heal our broken hearts. And sometimes we are given second chances. However it plays out for you, Hank, keep an open heart and keep believing in happy endings."

Hank knew the conversation he'd woken up remembering this morning was not likely exactly what Dorothy said on their last drive together. She'd told him that day of her long estrangement from her own son and how she'd almost let it break her. She said instead she had made herself walk in the door of a church one morning, determined to give whoever she sat beside the love they were missing.

Dorothy had indeed done that. With her generous spirit she'd given Hank the acceptance and true affection he had longed for from his own mother. He was able to forgive and let go of resentment and anger. Dorothy had loved Hank, and because of that he had been able to hang on long enough to receive love and forgiveness from his daughter and his grandson.

Believe in happy endings. Hank turned to look up again at the fifth-floor window. Jenny and Gloria had decided that for the next while he would live with Jenny during the week and go to Gloria's farmhouse on the weekends. Bruce and Liam had offered to step in whenever they were needed to help make things easier. No one was certain what Hank's needs would be in the next few months or how much longer he'd be given, but he would not face the end of his life alone.

Hank reached down under the table and traced his fingers along the stone arch, an original piece of the demolished church that now held the slab of polished stone. He stood and walked slowly to the sculpture, looking intently at the etched replica of the Gothic Arches and squinted to read the words.

This memorial was created to commemorate the
Centenary Queen Square United Church
which occupied this site from 1882–2019

Donated by the Wilbur Family

Hank's eyes focused on the archway of the blackened door and bowed his head in silent reverence.

Acknowledgements

Many thanks to my publisher, Terrilee Bulger. Once again, I thank editor Penelope Jackson profusely for her work and her passion. She pulled off the miraculous in this one. Thanks to designer and advocate Tracy Belsher. Thanks to Rudi Tusek for the interior design. Thanks to photographer Ian Mutto for taking just the right photograph which I believe captures the essence of this book. I am so appreciative of the way all these contributors supported my work.

I acknowledge the buildings, landmarks, people, and history of the city of Saint John. The seed of this story came from glancing into King's Square the first day I moved into my Princess Street apartment, and the story unfolded in the year I spent there.

Thanks to Wayne Harrison and Jim Boyd for their contributions.

I worked on this manuscript on my Go and Write retreat to London and the Cotswolds and appreciate Gerard Collins and Janie Simpson for making that such an amazing experience. Spending time in the company of passionate writers always helps to keep the writer in me motivated and on task.

I have such heartfelt gratitude for all my friends and family who support me daily. Thanks especially to my daughter Meg, who makes me laugh and keeps me humble. She is a loyal and vocal supporter of her mother's work. And to Burton whose love for and support of Mrs. White is constant.

Thanks for reading!

ACORNPRESS

Find more captivating titles on our website
acornpresscanada.com